Little Ghetto Girl
A Harlem Story
By
Danielle Santiago

PUBLISHED BY TWO OF A KIND
in association with MISCHIEVOUS GIRL INK

This reprinted edition has been professionally edited
by James B. Sims of inkeditor@aol.com

ISBN 0-9752589-0-7

Printed in the United States of America
Two of a Kind Publishing, Inc
3120 Milton Rd. Charlotte, NC
e-mail us at DanielleSantiago@twoofakindpublishing.com

*Rest In Peace Sharice Williams
We Miss You So Much.*

little ghetto girl (The song)
as rapped by Madam Sinclair

Verse one: Only one over twenty/ already seen and done plenty/ Absorbing my pains in this bottle of Henny/ My mind feel thirty I done lived that dirty/ And like Wayne the Lord knows I 'm not worthy/ Ol' schoolers say shorty wait for your glory/But it seems like troubles only waiting for me/From selling them trees to running them ki's/All the shit I done did out of impatience and greed/And sold my soul to the streets long ago/ and saw more Heat than any cop on beat/At night I can't sleep I'm in this game so deep/ I'm just a little ghetto girl running these streets.

Hook: Just a little Ghetto girl/ chasing dreams Of diamonds and pearls/ hustlin in to get by/Really lost in this cold world/

Verse two: And Niggas wanna know why ma stay on that shit/Cause I'm constantly wondering why I can't feel my clit/ Could it be from all them cocaine trips?/Wit that girly white inside my cho cha slit?/Town to town I'm making these niggas rich/Next time know what? This town I'll skip/Take a nigga yae and doe and make that shit flip/Now I trust no one not even my closest bitch/And I stay wit a loaded clip/ see how shit went with Po and Rich/ and the feds a have you on some real Gravano Gotti shit/divide and conquer your clique/last birthday I Made one wish/ to be as great as BIG and nice like Kiss/A bitch with a style so sick/ make prozac patients Flip and slit they wrist/
Chorus x3

Verse three: And now I'm hustling just to eat/ can you believe these Jealous bitches envy me?/ through all the shit the struggle and the strife/ I held you down, stayed your wife/ now you let the money make you trife/ and I guess you still blame me for losing our kid/ behind all the partying and bullshiting I did/ so now what I have to lose you too?/ so what! loss for a little ghetto girl ain't nothin new/ it's always apart of my world/ and my eternal chase for diamonds and pearls

Intro: How they began

The year was 2000 Kisa Montega was twenty-one, daring, and very attractive. Her skin was like caramel. Her eyes like chocolate, and her hair draped her face in a long doobie wrap.

Her wardrobe complimented her beauty; even her jeans and sneakers were Dolce and Gabbana, Gucci, or Prada.

To the public eye, when she maneuvered through downtown Manhattan, most thought she was an entertainer, model, or young businesswoman.

She was defiantly business minded, but quite the opposite of what they expected.

Her nickname was Kisa Kane and she happened to run the most lucrative cocaine business in Manhattan. With her sister and two cousins, the four were a deadly combination, their roots said it all, Black, Dominican, and South American.

Kisa and her sister Shea had not been raised together, because they did not have the same mother.

Years earlier Kisa had moved down south with their father and her mother to attend school. She had always returned to New York for the summer and holidays.

Kisa was closer to her two cousins, Eisani and TaTa, from her mother's side, than she was to her own sister. Kisa, TaTa, and Eisani looked like triplets when they were together.

Many joked that Kisa and Eisani had really been separated at birth. Both had the same hustling mentality, and the resemblance was eerie. Kisa had a lighter complexion with a more golden tone to her skin. Eisani was slimmer than her cousin was, and Kisa was six months older than Eisani.

Kisa's stint as a hustler began down south when she was in high school, selling dime bags of weed. She'd never imagined in her wildest dreams that it would come to this. Her future as a legitimate citizen seemed so bright, she excelled in academics and athletics. Believing she would go far with her many achievements, she moved back north for college.

Kisa attended Hunter College, while living in Harlem. She always dated or ran with hustlers, who could bless her with expensive gifts. She accepted the gifts, even though she could provide for herself with. Kisa ran with a thorough crew of guys, that had the streets uptown on lock, plus they pumped work into the surrounding boroughs. Kisa was like a little sister to them, and they were very protective of her. But some of them had secret fantasies about her.

All of her crewmembers had very profitable coke operations; it was through them that she'd gotten into the business. She started out simply delivering packages through the five boroughs for five hundred dollars a day.

Then it escalated to trafficking from state to state. From there she went to different islands picking up packages from suppliers; from there to running her own blocks in Harlem- all of this by the age of nineteen.

But the day after Kisa's twentieth birthday, things changed drastically. Sincere the boss of the family gave Kisa an elaborate party at the Carbon in downtown Manhattan. Everyone was there, from Mase to Mary J. Blige, to all the big hustlers from the five boroughs. You know the haters were there too, including all of the chicks that hated Kisa. She didn't give a damn though.

"Don't know. Don't care. Can't none of them beat my ass anyway." Were her exact words when Eisani asked her, "Why them bitches here, Kane?" Pointing out a group of girls from the Bronx she and Kisa had had beef with a few months earlier. Kisa could feel them watching her, so she partied even harder just to let them know she wasn't at all concerned with them.

The party was lavish but Sincere knew that nothing was too good for Kisa tonight. So he went all out-open bar, free bottles of Moet Chandon, Dom Perignon, and Cristal. He and Kisa had an on-again-off-again relationship. Sincere had plans on changing that. Tonight they were almost dressed alike in matching winter white leather; they hadn't even planned it. The two of them were just in sync with one another that much.

Kisa' s out fit was barely anything the shorts were so short, you would think she only had on a single-breasted jacket. Sincere kept it gully he wore a white Iceberg sweater, baggy white leather pants, a pair of fresh white uptowns (air force ones).

Kisa popped Cristal and danced the night away with any and everybody. Sincere just watched as niggas stuffed money and their phone numbers into her birthday bag. He was pissed, but there wasn't anything he could say; she wasn't his girl. When she chose him he didn't seem to choose her, so her attitude towards him was, "Fuck him!"

Eisani watched Sincere as he watched Kisa; she could see it in his face. Eisani walked over to Kisa's table. "Ma you know you making Sincere upset."
"And how am I doing that?"

"Don't look, but he's been watching you. And he see all these niggas in your face while you giving them your Miss America smile."

"He's not my man anyway. And just the way he see all that, I see all his bitches here at my party, all in his face."

Eisani sighed and walked away. She tried her best to get them together. Both of them loved each other so much, but neither wanted to get hurt again; so they were selfish with their feelings. And it didn't help that they were both as stubborn as mules.

Kisa looked to her right and caught Sincere staring. She got up, walked over to him, and wrapped her arm around him, knowing every chick was watching. She leaned in and whispered in his ear, "Baby what's the matter?"

"Nothing. Why you ask me that?"

"You over here looking at me all strange?"

"I was just watching all those fake-ass niggas all in your face."

"Why you worried about them? I'm not going home with them."

He gave her a sly smile, "Oh, word."

"That's my word, so you ready to go, pa?"

"Yeah let me get your drunk ass out of here before I have to hurt one of these niggas.

The next morning, Sincere woke Kisa up with the sweetest kisses and licks, until she almost came in his mouth, and that's right where he wanted her.

He pulled back and gently slid inside of her, placing one of her legs on his shoulder began stroking her slowly. She could only throw her head back and moan. He would make love to her slowly until they could climax together, or until Kisa starts speaking in Spanish. That always made Sincere come early no matter how hard he tried to fight it. She spared him and they came together. They were so exhausted they just lay in silence.

Kisa got up, showered, and then cooked breakfast. She bought the cheese eggs, steak and pancakes to the room on a tray and waited for Sincere to get out the shower.　He came out wrapped in a towel and saw the food, "Damn I must have dicked you down good!　I ain't never got breakfast."

"You never been here past eight o' clock in the morning."

"Come on, ma, don't start that.　I'm here now." He sat down on the opposite side of the bed and reached in the nightstand drawer next to the bed.　He pulled out four boxes.

Kisa's eyes lit up.　It was the love of her life-jewelry!　She snatched the boxes from him.　The first box contained a platinum diamond baguette necklace, with a hidden setting.　In the second box was a matching bracelet.

When Kisa reached for the third box, Sincere snatched the fourth box away.　In this box was a pair of matching earrings.　All three pieces were beautiful. They all were custom-made.　When she reached for the last box, Sincere shook his head.

"Come on, Sin, give me the box, stop bullshittin'."

"This ain't no bullshit.　The only way you can have this box is, if you agree to be wifey!"

The next thirty seconds seemed like an eternity. Everything through her head: She had saved plenty of money; she had a nice coop in Esplanade Gardens, a 1999 4.6 Range Rover; a very nice lucrative hair salon on 125th Street.　Now she was ready to get out of the game, with the RICO and Rockefeller laws in full effect niggas was getting knocked right and left.　Not to mention the snitches, the jealous hoes, and even more the stickup kids.　One question stuck out in her mind: *Would being his wife really take her out of the game?　Or would it make matters worse?*

Kisa wasn't naive; she knew how niggas got down when it came to street shit and handling it. She knew the first thing they loved to do was kidnap someone's wife to get what they wanted.

Sincere stood over Kisa, staring at her. He finally interrupted her train of thought. "Did I ask you the twenty thousand dollar question or something?"

Snapping out of her trance she replied, "I was just thinking how I've been wanting to get out of the game. The jail time and the danger stay on my mind. And if I become your wife, the even more dangerous it would be for me."

He just looked at her and smiled; this was one of the things he loved about her. She was a strategist always thinking on her feet. "Look Kane I know we've had our bouts in the past, but I always knew you were the one. I planned this months before I ever thought about giving you a birthday party. Last night really got to me watching those niggas drool over you, like I wasn't there." He grabbed her hand. "I always respected your space, because I never officially gave you the title of being my girl. You've always been loyal to me, never messed with any of my friends. You've always been able to take care of yourself, so I know you not after my paper like all those other gold-digging bitches. All I'm trying to say is if I have you, everything in my life will be complete."

"But, Sincere, baby, how much longer do you have to keep dealing in the streets. We both have more than enough saved to leave all this street shit alone and run our legit businesses."

"You know it's not that simple for me to get out, ma. Just say yes, and you never have to play the streets as long as I'm around. I don't know what you're worried about someone stepping to you. Shit, I've seen you hold your own, the way you blaze that .380 at those stickup kids that day. Stop fronting like you not nice with yours shorty."

She knew that there was nothing else to say. She sat on his lap, hugged his neck, and said, "Of course I'll be your wife."

Sincere opened the box. The ring was five karats, baguettes and solitaires set in platinum.

They had made love all day, completely forgetting about cell phones, pagers, or any connections with the outside world.

By the end of the day, they lay in sweat and juices, holding each other. Sharing the same thought, *finally together.*

Track 2: Street Sweepers

The last year had been as wonderful as Sincere had promised Kisa it would be. She didn't play the streets anymore, but she was still well informed about the business. Now she was focused on college, in addition to her hair salon, she opened a full-service day spa.

Life was cocaine; she was able to send her mother a very large sum of money for Christmas. She took care of anything her little sister and brother needed for their college education, even though they were still in high school. She loved them more than life it self. She always told the both of them, "Anything you need come to me. As long as you're doing good in school I'll give it to you."

Kisa was adamant about them not living the street life. She took another portion of her savings and invested in CDs, mutual funds, and the stock market. She was really enjoying life to the fullest. Her and Sincere took trips to the islands, which she enjoyed thoroughly, because now it was all pleasure.

No business to worry about.   No more lining luggage with petroleum-dipped kilos, and the dread of going through customs.

Kisa's twenty-first birthday was approaching fast. Sincere wanted to throw her a big bash, Kisa firmly objected, "Even though we're not legally married, I want to celebrate my birthday and our one year anniversary alone.   As a matter of fact, I made reservations for us at a little ski resort in Maine."

What Kisa wanted, Kisa got.   Plus Sincere enjoyed the little surprises she kept in store for him. He had to be careful when he brought his friends to the house.   Kisa had a knack for sitting in the house ass naked with a pair of stilettos on, when he got home.   Sometimes she would put on her floor length chinchilla, with only a bra and thong underneath. She would hop in her Range just like that and drive to the block to pick him up.

Sincere smiled to himself thinking, *my baby is such an undercover freak.* "Sure I need to get away, shit is going crazy right now."

Kisa was geeked that she would have her man to herself for the first time in months.

After thanking him with some toe-curling head, she showered and prepared to go shopping for their trip. She walked back into the room and saw him in the bed she thought *I knew after that top I gave him he would be in a deep sleep.* She began to kiss him softly and massage his dick until he woke up with an erection. He thought his mommy was about to give him some cho-cha. He pulled her down into the bed, wondering why she was fully dressed. "Where do you think you're going, lil mama?"

"I'm going to Garden State Plaza, then to the city to pick up a couple of things. I don't have any cash and I wanted to drive the five."

"Oh but what you gonna do about what you started?" He asked looking down at his erect penis.

"I promise, poppi, I'll make it up to you tonight."

"That's your word?"

"That's my word, my nigga."

With that he handed her the keys to the five hundred and gave her four dollars. Kisa kissed him and told him "Keep your cell on; I don't want to hear shit about your battery being dead. One."

Sincere just looked at his woman as she walked away, admiring the way her Sergio's hugged her big ass and wide hips. Her waist was so small it looked as if a cantaloupe was sitting on top of a watermelon. In his mind she was the total package: She took good care of him mentally, physically, and emotionally. That's why he gave her whatever she wanted, right down to that $850,000 townhouse, right across the water in Jersey. It was positioned so perfectly; you could see Manhattan while looking out the window.

He knew Kisa knew about his other girls. Shit, they damn near chased her down to let her know! Leaving notes on her truck and even keying it. They even called her from time to time. At first she would spaz out and threatened to leave. Then he would just do something really special for her or buy her something expensive.

Finally Kisa stopped taking the gifts and flat out refused to hear anything he had to say. He soon got the picture, so he slowed his roll. His sideline bitches really stopped messing with Kisa after she pistol-whipped Toki, a bum-ass bitch Sincere had gotten pregnant. He made her have an abortion. Toki was foolish enough to discuss the abortion and Sincere with her friend Neka, while waiting to get their hair done at Kisa's salon. She was doing it purposely and loudly, because this was one of the very few times Kisa was in the salon. "That nigga Sin ain't shit. Hell he paid me five thousand dollars to get rid of the baby, when he knocked me up! She walking around here like she got something good. Please that bastard fucking everything from 110th to 155th. Between the eastside and Westside."

By then everyone in the shop was getting nervous; they all knew Kisa wasn't playing with a full deck. Kisa's little cousin, Tyies, who worked in the salon asked Kisa "Kane, do you want me to toss these cackling hoes out of here?"

Kisa stated loudly, "I don't give a fuck about no five thousand dollar hoe! Shit is that all she is worth?

I got the ring, the house, the cars, and the man. So fuck that miserable beat walking bitch!"

Toki jumped up and told Kisa, "No bitch you the miserable one!"

Before Toki could get another word out of her mouth, Kisa had pulled a curling iron from the nearest stove, and smacked her across the right side of her face, branding Toki permanently. The fight was over. Then Kisa pushed her out of the door and onto the sidewalk.

Neka acted as if she wanted to jump in. Kisa turned around and pulled out a .380 from the small of her back. Neka quickly left that shit alone.

Toki rushed back inside, not realizing Kisa had the gun; she swung on Kisa but missed. Kisa grabbed her arm, put it behind her back and beat her with the gun. After five hits Toki was down.

Tyeis stashed the gun in her car. When Kisa was arrested she was only charged with assault, because the police couldn't find the gun, and no one in the shop would back up Toki and Neka's claim about the it.

Kisa's bail was only one thousand dollars. When Sincere picked her up, she smacked him in the face, and told him, "Its your fault all this shit is happening, all because you can't keep your dick in your pants!"

He quickly defended himself by saying, "All that stuff that bitch, Toki, was talking about was before we got together! I'm serious!"

Kisa didn't care. She was fed up. She moved back to her apartment. Sincere didn't know she'd kept it. He begged and pleaded for her to come home. After two months she was back in Jersey. That was one episode Sincere really wanted to forget.

As Kisa drove to the mall she paid close attention to a black truck in her rearview mirror. It had been behind her for about fifteen minutes. Her suspicions were on high alert when she began looking for a parking space.

Every row she turned on, the truck followed. She finally found parking in the upper-level deck next to Neiman Marcus. Thinking it might be stickup kids, she reached for the Ruger, which Sincere kept in a hidden compartment, and put it in her Prada knapsack.

As she walked away from the car, she noticed the truck parked two rows over. Once she got a good look at the license plate her worries of a stick-up were put to rest. It was only the NYPD.

In the truck was a team of investigators called the Street-Sweepers. Their assignment was to bring down all the major heroin and cocaine dealers in the five boroughs. The team had already successfully taken down three of the city's most notorious drug rings. They had not been able to take down Sincere's team, due to the fact that four of the eight-member team was on Sincere's payroll.

The team had mistakenly followed Kisa thinking she was Sincere. The tints on the Benz were so dark they could not tell the difference until she exited the car.

When Kisa entered the mall she immediately called Sincere. "The jakes followed me to the mall; I didn't see them come in though."

He told her, "Just keep on doing what you were doing. Act normal; you not doing shit wrong anyway. Call me when you leave the mall, and let me know if they're still following you. I'm already in the city taking care of some business."

Actually the street sweepers were long gone, pissed that they'd followed Kisa instead of Sincere. They had a tip that Sincere had a big deal going down on this particular Friday.

Sincere was vexed that neither Santangelo, Warren, McNeely, nor Smith had informed him about this. They were the four detectives on his payroll. He paid them each what the four of them made together for one year.

The team usually got briefed in the office before beginning surveillance. Today was different. There was a late tip, and Captain Moyarty had his suspicions about there being a leak on his team. It was just Sincere's luck that Kisa drove the Benz today.

Kisa walked into the parking deck and look around for the police. She looked down at her watch and couldn't believe how much time had gone by. The three hours seemed like an hour. She picked up her phone to call Eisani they were supposed to meet an hour earlier. "Yo E what up?"

"Ain't nothing. Where the hell you at? You was supposed to meet me an hour ago, and I been calling your phone!"

"Ma, some crazy shit happened on the way to the mall today, but I will tell you about that when I see you. That threw me off so I lost track of time, but I'm on the way. Where you at?"

"I'm already downtown at Louis Vuitton. I caught a cab, so just tell me where you want to meet at and I'll be there."

"Meet me in thirty minutes in the Village in front of Petit Peton."

"Aight, that's straight. One."

"One."

When Kisa pulled up in front of Petit Peton there was her cousin, the closest person to her in the world besides Sincere. She stood with her hand on her hip like she had an attitude and a smirk on her face. She was dressed nicely for the unusually warm winter day in an Emillio Pucci blouse, a pair Chloe jeans, and a brown Christian Dior jacket with the matching boots and bag.

Kisa parked and walked over to her, they affectionately greeted each other at the same time, "Hey bitch." That's how they greeted one another, to them it was an appropriate and normal greeting.

Kisa stepped back and gave her cousin a once over, "Looking good ma, I like."

"Girl please, anyway what are you coming down here to buy now? You do not need anymore boots."

"No girl you have not seen these, they are the flyest boots I have to have them."

"Kane you have a terrible shoe fetish, you need help." They both fell out in laughter.

As they walked into the store, the staff gave Kisa the royal treatment. They saw her almost on a weekly basis and they knew she was coming with one plan to spend money. Petit Peton was her favorite shoe store in the city they carried some of the most exclusive shoes and boots in the Village. Kisa's favorite salesmen Bobby walked over and greeted her. "Hey Ms. Thing, what are you looking for today?"

"I'm not shopping today baby, they called and said the boots I ordered were here."

"Let me go get them and look over there we have a new collection just in today."

"I'll check it out thanks." Kisa turned around and began to speak, but stopped short when she didn't see Eisani. She walked to the entrance and saw Eisani talking to a very fine guy. She looked on until Bobby came back with her boots. "Here is your order, do you want to try them on?"

"No Bobby you can just throw them in a bag and I will be on my way."

"Did you like anything in the collection?"

"I really didn't get a good look at it but I will the next time."

Bobby handed Kisa her bag and she was on her way to see who her cousin was in deep conversation with. She walked over and stood next to Eisani, "E who is your friend?"

"Kane, this is Elijah, and Elijah, this is my cousin Kane."

He was in awe at how much they looked alike. He reached out and shook Kisa's hand.

"The two of you share such a strong resemblance I would swear you were sisters, twin sisters."

The two of them were use to this, in unison they answered, "We get that all the time."

"I'm sure you do, well I don't want to hold your shopping spree up. I know how you ladies are about that and I have to get back to Brooklyn anyway. Eisani I will call you maybe we can get something to eat later."

Eisani who was blushing red answered with a slight giggle in her voice, "Okay sweetie, I'll hit you when I'm done with all my errands."

"That's straight, be careful out here, and it was nice meeting you Kane."

"You too Elijah, bye-bye." Kisa walked to the car as Eisani and Elijah said their good byes. As soon as Eisani got in the car Kisa started asking questions about Elijah.

"So how long have you known him?"

"We have been seeing each other about two months."

"And when were you going to tell me chic?"

"I was just waiting for the right time, I just feel him so much Kane. And you know how that shit goes, as soon as I start telling everybody it will fall off."

"Ma please! He is a cutie though, where did y'all meet?"

"Girl I had to go to BK one day to drop off some work to my cousin, somewhere I rarely venture. Any way when I came out the building it was a whole entourage of niggas standing on the corner. So you know they was calling out to me with that yo shorty come here shit, you know the usual. So I ignored them and got in the truck. Then Elijah came over to the truck before I could pull off. He said some old fly shit and the rest is history, we went out that night and we have been hanging tight ever since."

"No wonder I can't ever find your fast ass at night. So you went and got you a Brooklyn nigga, I hear that fly shit ma."

"You know me bitch, I'm versatile these days."

"So what does he do?"

"You know I always attract guys who are in the game too. But he fuck with more than girl, he is into a little bit of everything."

"Word."

"Yea he is definitely doing his thing in BK and a couple of other places."

They shopped for hours and talked about the state of their personal lives. Their last stop was Bergdorf Goodman after they left Kisa called to check in with Sincere. He was happy to hear from her, "What up baby?"

"Nothing poppi, just calling to see what's good with you?"

"I'm uptown chilling and why didn't you call me when you left the mall."

"Cause when I came out, they were gone and I had forgot that E was waiting on me downtown. So basically I got sidetracked."

"Is that so? Where you going now?"

"I'm on my way uptown I need to stop at the Apollo Express."

"After you finish there meet me in front of the mart, I didn't drive Mannie picked me up."

"Well give me about forty-five minutes, Love you"

"Love you too."

Kisa and Eisani finished shopping and started to cross the street to meet Sincere. From where they stood they could see Sincere, his entire crew plus about ten additional niggas. What really caught Kisa's attention, was the six girls they were talking to. Especially the tall, thick, pecan tanned girl in Sincere's face. Eisani did not pay any attention to what was going on across the street until she noticed Kisa quickening her step. Kisa did not have to say anything to Eisani about what she was witnessing. She knew in any situation if she started throwing punches, Eisani was coming right behind her with no questions.

Sincere never saw Kisa coming, he looked up and she was standing next to the girl.

"Who the fuck is this bitch you all yackety yacketing wit?"

The girl interrupted, "Who are you calling a bitch?"

The younger guys gas the situation, but Sincere's main men knew not to instigate it. They all knew what Kisa was capable of. Kisa looked at the girl and could tell she was soft and only spoke up because her girls were with her.

"Bitch mind your business, cause this right here is mine." She said pointing to Sincere.

Eisani stepped in between the girl and Kisa, "So that means beat your feet bitch."

Although they outnumbered Kisa and Eisani by four, they were from Queens. And they didn't want to start some shit in another borough, not knowing how deep their opponents rolled. Even more they had to worry about the guys jumping in. They walked away and Kisa turned to Sincere, "So you starting with the Bitches again?"

"Come on Kane don't start, I was only talking to that broad, I don't even know her. You always spazzin over nothing."

"That's always the story Sin when I catch you. Oh but let a nigga even look at me the wrong way, you scream on me."

"Come on Kane you're making a scene where is the car?"

Kisa walked off leaving him to walk behind her with Eisani.

They dropped Eisani off at her apartment and headed for the bridge. Kisa looked out the window and said nothing for the entire ride to Jersey. When they got home she cooked dinner. She fixed Sincere's plate and served it to him in the den instead of the dinning room.

"Why did you bring my plate in here?"

She ignored him and proceeded to walk out the room, Sincere called out to her with authority,

"Kisa I know you hear me talking to you, come here."

She stopped in her tracks he only called her Kisa when it was serious. She walked back in the

Den and leaned against the bar with an attitude. Sincere knew she was being stubborn so he walked over to her and got in her face.

"Ma come on let that shit go it was nothing. I don't want to beef with you tonight. You know I love you." He wrapped his arms around her and squeezed her tight. They had been together a year, but his hugs still made her feel warm and secure. She couldn't fight it anymore,

"I love you too Sincere."

He kissed her forehead, her nose, and then her mouth. He was an excellent kisser he gently stroked her lips with soft licks. Then he slid his tongue in and out of her mouth. He placed one gentle kiss on her chin, and kisses all over her neck.

He unbuttoned her shirt and massaged her breast. He pulled her jeans off and placed her on the bar. He pulled her thong to the side, and slid inside of her. He pushed her knees all the way back to her shoulders and began thrusting in and out of her, causing her to moan loudly with pleasure.

Her body tingled all over as he pulled out and flipped her onto her stomach, closed her legs and slid back in. He began stroking her so fast she couldn't hold back any longer, she came so hard she wet up his jeans and the bar.

Sincere couldn't fight it anymore he came so hard it took all of his energy. After a few minutes he got off the bar, pulled Kisa down and led her to the bedroom. They made love all night, the best kind of love, make up love.

Three days later when Sincere and Kisa were preparing to go to the airport, all hell broke loose. Sincere was sitting in the living room with his right hand men Butta, Shawn, and Mannie going over how everything would be ran while Sincere was in Maine. All of a sudden there was a loud bang on the front door, and a lot of screaming. Everyone's first thought was a robbery, then they saw the NYPD and NJ State Police jackets and new it was a raid.

Once again Sincere felt like he had been shitted on by the cops he paid to keep him informed. As the cops rushed through the house purposely knocking things over, Sincere and his crew stood still hands raised in the air, knowing the best thing to do was to cooperate. As the cop's handcuffed each man, Detective Santangelo made sure he was the one to grab Sincere and search him. Santangelo saw the look in Sincere's eyes, so he made sure Sincere was put in his car so he could talk to him.

Once he placed Sincere in his car, Santangelo walked back into the house. Sincere grew even madder when he saw two officers bringing Kisa out in handcuffs. He could not tell how she was feeling, for her face showed no emotions. At this moment she still looked gorgeous to him, she looked prepared for a ski trip in her cream Prada ski suit and parka, not a jail cell.

Inside Kisa was furious, but she knew there was no one to blame but herself and Sincere. And she really could not blame him, she had her own mind and she chose to stay.

Track 3: New York, New York

The police released Kisa , after she played her dumb girlfriend role. They really thought she didn't know anything, and they hadn't had her on any surveillance. Kisa had stopped dealing four months before they began following Sincere and his team.

On the way to the precinct, Santangelo had informed Sincere that they knew nothing about the raid until five minutes before suiting up.

"Sincere, I promise you, only the captain and his assistant knew. The old Cap doesn't trust anyone right now. He knows there is a leak on his team; until he figures out who it is shit's going to be tight. I'll try my best to tamper with some of the evidence, but I can't promise you anything."

Sincere responded calmly, "I pay you muthafuckas too much for this shit to happen. And Kisa does not have anything to do with this. I don't want her spending more than forty-five minutes in the station. I know there was nothing in the house, so you don't have anything to hold her on."

Sincere was so frustrated, he caught a migraine he just laid his head back against the seat and analyzed the situation. He had worked too hard building his operation to let a team full of corrupt cops take it down.

Sincere had started moving cocaine at the age of thirteen. He was a humble kid. The old school heads respected him and looked out for him, for simple reasons: He was smart, very respectful, and he listened intently when they gave him advice.

He wasn't a hot head like a lot of young guys in the late eighties and early nineties, running around killing each other just because they could. He was always peaceful unless he had no other alternative. He minded his business and stuck to getting his paper.

By fifteen he had a connect that sold him ounces of cocaine for short money. He was moving around five to ten ounces a week. He sold coke by the ounce, grams, or cooked up, and he ran two blocks around his way.

He was sixteen bringing home better than six thousand dollars a week in a single mother home. What could his mother say? It wasn't that she couldn't pay the bills; she always held her own, and as a child, Sincere never wanted for anything.

But she didn't say anything, because she knew hustling came natural to Sincere. It was in his blood. Her own father was a made man in La Costa Nostra, and Sincere's father worked hand in hand with PeeWee Kirkland. He never knew his father but acted just like him in all his ways and movements.

His father had been killed before Sincere was born. Killed in a shoot out on Broadway in the middle of the day. By the time he was nineteen his Italian grandfather introduced to a new connect, taking business to another level. From that point, there was no turning back. He was buying and moving five kilos a week.

That was seven years ago. Now he was twenty-six with a coke operation worth well over twenty million dollars a year. All he wanted was another three years with no interruptions and he would get out.

He owned two barbershops, one in Harlem and one in the Bronx. He also owned a corner store, and a beauty supply store in Harlem. He had been to jail before when TNT took him off the block. But he had never had his home raided.

He knew that this time they must have gotten some pretty serious evidence on him in order to get a warrant to raid his home across state lines. All he could think about at that moment was the look on Kisa's face when the jake's were taking her away.

As Kisa walked out of the interrogation room, Shea got up and gave her sister a hug. They had a brief conversation.

Kisa walked over to the station desk to retrieve her belongings. The middle-aged white man working the desk looked at them with disgust, especially at Shea. She was dressed to the Tee; in black leather riding pants, a black mohair sweater, and a deep brown swing mink coat with a matching head wrap.

When Kisa asked for her belongings, the man's attitude was blatant towards her. Once he handed her the envelope, she emptied the contents on the counter to make sure everything was there.

The man could not take his eyes off the jewelry that lay on the counter. He knew it was worth more than his salary for two years. He just rolled his eyes at her and walked off.

When Kisa and Shea exited the station, members of the street team were standing around smoking cigarettes. Kisa could hear them whispering behind her.

She turned around and asked them, "Why the fuck are you all whispering like little bitches? Fuck your corrupt pig-asses anyway. I'll be back for my husband tomorrow, and not a hair on his head better be out of place."

They all stood there not believing she had just showed such blatant disrespect towards them she and Shea pulled off in a cherry red CLK.

When Kisa saw the inside of her house the tears rolled down her face. Everything that was breakable had been broken. All her sofas and mattresses had been cut up, and the inside of every car had been virtually destroyed.

She looked at Shea and asked her, "What am I gonna do?"

"First we're going to salvage what clothes and furniture we can. So I'm going to run to K-mart and get some storage bins for the clothes. While I'm gone you take a hot shower, and get me out a T-shirt and some sweats so we can get to work when I get back."

When Shea was out the front door Kisa turned on the shower and began to undress, *I'm supposed to be spending a romantic week with my man, in a cozy cabin.*

But this was her reality. When she stepped out of the shower, the phone was ringing. She ran to pick it up, and it was Sincere on the other end.

"Baby, you okay? I know they didn't fuck with you, did they?"

"No, baby, I'm fine. How are you holding up? Are they saying when they're going to release you?"

"We should be arraigned tomorrow. My lawyer is out of town. He's flying back tonight and he said he's coming straight here."

"Sin, you know they completely fucked the house and the cars up! So I'm going to pack up some stuff and take it to Esplanade. She said with stress in her voice. "The furniture is useless so I'm just going to have someone come move this shit out. By the way, how much money was in the safe?"

"Only a couple of thousand, Why?"

"Because it's empty. And they cut up my chinchilla and your white mink. I'll take them to the furrier to see if they can be repaired."

She waited for a response, but he was silent. "I'm going to have the tow trucks come out and pick up the cars to be repaired in the morning. Do you want me to have Shawn and Mannie's car picked up too?"

"Yeah, you might as well. Look I have to go now. I want you to keep a piece with you. And I want TaTa, Eisani, or Shea to stay with you. Be careful, I love you ma, I'll be home soon."

"Sure baby I love you too. Keep your head up poppi. One."

It would be seven o'clock the next morning before Kisa and Shea finished cleaning and packing everything. Once they put everything in order they decided to go to breakfast. While they were at IHOP, Kisa made arrangements with her lawyer to meet at the house. She also made arrangements for all the cars to be towed. Kisa sat at the table and picked over her food.

Shea sat and stared at her younger sister. Then Shea sparked the conversation with a question. "Ma what are you going to do if they don't let Sincere out?"

Kisa stared back at Shea coldly. "What do you mean *if they don't let Sincere out?*" she responded with a very aggravated look on her face.

"I'm just saying, are you prepared to live without that nigga?"

"Yo Shea you talking like you know something I don't know. What's poppin? Let me in, big sis." Kisa said with a sarcastic smirk on her face.

Shea enjoyed giving her sister the I-told-you-so lectures. "Well, if you'd brought your lil' bourgeois ass back to the hood sometimes, you would hear some things!"

"Bitch, who are you calling bourgeois? Just 'cause I got better shit to do than run around Eighth Ave. all the time and cluck like we go to P.S. 89, or gossip all day with them project bitches, it doesn't mean I'm bourgeois. And further more, I'm only twenty-one with three businesses to run and I'm trying to go to college. And right now I really don't need your fucking sarcasm!"

By now everyone in the restaurant was staring at them.

"If you shut your little ass up, I can tell you what I know," Shea told Kisa.

Kisa closed her mouth, folded arms across her chest, and waited for Shea to begin.

"Supposedly, there were some little young niggas from the East Side on the come up. For the last couple of months they had been taking over major spots and just bodying niggas all over Harlem. Mannie's lil' cousin Jo-Jo, happened to work for Carlos, the guy who leads these young niggas." Shea took a sip from her coffee.

"Panamanian Carlos from Grant projects. Isn't he dead?"

"Yeah."

"What in the hell does he have to do with Sincere's case."

"If you shut the fuck up, I can finish."

Kennedy rolled her eye. *I should reach over there, and smack that stupid smirk off her face. Hold your composure Kane; so you can find out what is going on.* "Aight finish then."

"When Jo-Jo found out Carlos had plans to take over Sincere's spots, he told Mannie. Sincere began paying Jo-Jo to keep him informed. Jo-Jo told Sin that

Carlos would be sending people to get real cool with him so they could infiltrate his team. When that plan didn't work, Carlos began paying people to find out where y'all lived. It just so happened that one night when Sincere was on his way home, he noticed someone following him." Shea looked around. "Sincere called Terry, Butta, Shawn, and Mannie and told them to meet him. He led the car into a trap." She hesitated. "Word on the street is Sincere and them tortured Carlos's henchmen until they told him what he wanted to know. Then Sincere merked them niggas and put them back in the truck and parked it in front of 1199. That's Carlos's building. Now that shit made Carlos furious. So he made plans to have you kidnapped. When Sincere heard that, he went seven-thirty. The next day, Sincere and them ran right up in Los spot and did every nigga in there dirty, but they only killed Carlos. So I know for a fact your boo-boo is in that cell praying that he wasn't under surveillance on any of those days."

Kisa sat in astonishment. She had no clue about any of this. *How could Sin keep something this serious from me?* "Shea, why didn't you tell me about this?"

"At first I thought you knew, then Shawn told me Sin didn't want you to know anything. He didn't want to scare you. Shawn said they just had security follow you around, in case anything jumped off."

Kisa was disgusted that Shea had one up on her.

"Well, I'll deal with Sincere later. Come on. I have to get back to the house now."

When Kisa and Shea pulled up to the house, Kisa saw her lawyer, Mrs. Bovani. She was sending two disappointed New Jersey State policemen away.

Kisa stepped out the car to greet her.

"Hi.   Thanks for coming out on such short notice. What did those jakes want?"

"Those cops were here to confiscate your cars and home, but after you had told me what happened, I prepared the appropriate paper work. I showed them papers that indicated that the house and cars were in your name.   Your profits from your business, proves you make enough to pay for your properties. Also here are the records you requested."

"Thanks, Mrs. Bovani.   That's exactly what I needed these records for. I just never imagined they would come so soon. Would you like to come in and have something to drink? It's a bit messy. We cleaned and packed up what we could."

"No, thanks, baby I have to be going now. If you need anything else, call me at anytime."

"I most certainly will. Thanks again. Bye-bye."

As soon as Kisa opened the door the phone was ringing. She ran to answer it. "Hello?"

"What up, baby?"

It was Sincere. His voice sounded emotional and sad.

"Hi, Sin. How are you holding up?"

"I'm aight. My lawyer just left."

"Well what did he say?"

"He said these jakes ain't trying to give me no bail!"

"What?"

"Yeah, they on some real bullshit, talking about bringing the Feds in since I live across state lines. I'll just see what happens when I go to court tonight. I need you to come down here with some type of money just in case I get a bail."

"Baby, you know I'll be there regardless. Anyway, you know the cops came by here trying to confiscate shit, but I was on top of things. The jakes was dumb heated when they couldn't take our stuff."

"Yeah, Kane, I heard about that little presentation you put on last night when you were leaving the precinct. Ma I know you was upset and all, but that really doesn't help the situation right now. You have to learn to control those fuckin' temper tantrums. Aight?"

"Yeah, whatever." Kisa responded dryly, "Anyway, I'm going to forward the house phone to my cell phone. Call me when you find out what time you are going to be in court."

Kisa's tone sounded as if she was really uninterested.

"Yo, Kane, why you gotta sound like that? And who said I was through talking to you anyway?"

"Sin, what else do you have to say that you can say over the phone?"

"Ma, what's with the fucking attitude? I should have the attitude; I'm the one locked up!"

"And whose fault is that, Sin?"

"Yo, let me get off this phone. I'll see you tonight, 'cause right now you on some fly shit. And when I see you I'm gonna smack the shit out of your ass!"

"Whatever Sin, holla."

Sincere was steaming when he hung up the phone. *I'm not even gonna let Kane stress me today. Her ass just mad cause we didn't go on the trip.*

Kisa knew she was wrong but she didn't care. *Fuck Sincere. All the shit I go through, with him. I deserve to have an attitude. Plus he kept the Carlos shit from me.*

"Yo, Shea, lets go to The World. I need to go shopping, and I need to stop and get some money from the safe in the salon before stupid-ass has to be in night court."

Shea walked into the room. "Why is he a stupid ass now? And twenty minutes ago he was your baby."

"Because he is an asshole. Plain and simple."

"Damn! What's done crawled up your ass?" Shea asked.

"Nothing. Let's just get out of this house."

Once Shawn had called his baby's mother, Shamique from jail, and told her about the raid, everybody in Harlem knew. Kisa was said, "Damn that bitch must be the ghetto gazette or something."

Once she and Shea hit the sidewalk on 125th street, every guy who was associated with Sincere stopped Kisa and asked about him. They wanted to know if he or she needed anything.

Kisa was polite, but she kept it moving. She knew most of them had ulterior motives.

Kisa walked into the Apollo Express. The owner, Miss Mary, flashed a big smile. She wasn't smiling just because Kisa was a good customer; She really liked her.

Kisa was nice, and she wasn't stuck up like a lot of the drug dealer's girlfriends, or the girls who had a little money and could afford to shop in her store. Kisa would bring Miss Mary lunch, and gift certificates from her salon.

Today Miss Mary wanted to see how Kisa was holding up, because, of course, she had heard about Sincere.

As always, Kisa gave Mary a big hug.

"Hi, Miss Mary. How are you?"

"No, baby, how are you? I heard what happened to Sin."

"Who hasn't heard? But we're doing as fine as could be expected. That's why I'm in here today. I need something to wear to night court. You know them jakes fucked up a lot of our clothes. I just need something casual but not too plain."

"Well, baby, pick out whatever you need, and you know I'll give you a good deal. And, little Miss Shea when was you going to speak?"

"Well, hell, I didn't think y'all was ever going to stop chit-chattin"

"Girl, please. You don't even come see me anymore. You big time now? My store ain't good enough no more?"

"Nah, Miss Mary, you know it ain't that. I don't need anything else. I'm already running out of closet space."

"Well, while your sister is shopping, I just got this beautiful mink ski suit in that I know you will love."

Kisa had a very bad shopping habit. She could not just go in and get what she needed. If she saw something extra she had to have it. She settled for a pair of beige Fendi pants and matching top, with a long cream Coogi wrap. She decided that's what she would wear to court. Then she saw a pair of Damier Louis Vuitton boots she had to have, along with four packs of monogram Gucci pantyhose, and a couple Coogi dresses with the new patterns.

When Kisa got up to the register, Shea just looked at her and said, "You need to stop."

"Look, you know I need these things. You saw how my clothes was messed up."

"You act like you don't have a big-ass closet in Esplanade. But whatever ma. Do you." Shea hissed.

Kisa spotted a coat that she was dying for. "Miss Mary what's up wit that red fox up there?"

Shea quickly interrupted. "No, Miss Mary, tell her she don't need it."

"Shea, shut up! You saw how they killed my coats; my chinchilla probably can't even be fixed. Can I try that coat on, please?"

"Sure, baby, and Shea, leave your sister alone; let her get whatever she needs."

When Kisa put the coat on, she was radiant, and the coat totally complimented her complexion. Shea looked on with a flicker of envy in her eyes; She knew her sister was gorgeous, but the clothes and jewelry just made her glamorous.

In that short ten minutes Kisa had spent ten thousand dollars on clothes.

"Alright!" she exclaimed. "I'm outta here, I'm spending cash like I don't have to pay a nigga bail."

Mary thanked Kisa for coming in. "And you know I'll have the new spring stuff in next week," she added.

"And you know I'll be here. Oh can you order me another Coogi bedspread and check on a black mink bedspread?"

"Sure, baby, and Tell Sin it will work out. I'm praying for him."

Kisa and Shea were in court by eight o'clock. Sincere's case was called at nine-thirty. In Kisa's eyes, the prosecutor was a real asshole. Everyone was charged with conspiracy to traffic and distribute a controlled substance, and carrying illegal firearms.

Sincere was also charged with operating a criminal enterprise.

Mr. McDougall, the prosecutor, informed the judge that the defendants were also being investigated for a series of homicides and home invasions in Manhattan and New Jersey, and he wanted the judge to take that into consideration and set bail at one million dollars for each defendant.

The judge looked at McDougall, and asked, "Have they been charged with any of these other alleged crimes?"

"No your Honor," he answered.

"Then I'm not taking it into consideration. Were there any narcotics found at the time of the raid on the premises?"

"No but there were illegal firearms confiscated."

Mazetti abruptly contested,

"Your honor they were not illegal arms they were simply not registered."

"Well, bail is set at forty-five thousand dollars apiece."

Kisa was smiling so hard she could barley contain herself from laughing. She had already called the bail bondsman and he was waiting for her at the back of the courtroom. Kisa walked over to him and opened her Fendi bag pulling out one of five envelopes, each containing twenty thousand dollars. She smiled at the short balding man.

"Hi, Macky. Here is ten percent for each one of them, and you can keep the extra two thousand for coming out personally on such short notice. I know you are such a busy man." Kisa winked at him. He was blushing so hard his face was red.

"Now, Kane, you know that's not necessary. Thanks for your consideration. I need you to come with me to sign these papers and I'll have Sin out in no time."

Kisa was standing outside of TaTa's Navigator, while Shea and TaTa sat in Shea's CLK talking. When Sincere walked out and saw Kisa standing there, he forgot all about their earlier disagreement.

He grabbed her and hugged her tight.

"Baby, I'm so glad to see you"

"No, bay, I'm glad to see you, and I'm sorry I acted so ugly on the phone. I was just so frustrated. You know I love you." By now Kisa had tears streaming down her face.

"Ma, stop crying."

"Yeah," remarked Butta, "and give me a hug too!"

Sincere shot him a look. *Get your own, nigga.*

"Shit, she looking all warm wit that fox on. Its freezing out here, and them stupid-ass jakes didn't let us take our coats."

Sincere looked at Butta. "Well get your monkey ass in the truck, nigga."

Everyone climbed in the truck and headed up the West Side highway to Harlem. Everyone shared his or her point of view on the raid and getting out of jail. In the car behind them, Shea and TaTa smoked a blunt filled with Branson, while listening to Biggie's *Born Again* CD. TaTa skipped to number seventeen, while taking a big toke off the blunt.

"Oh this is my *shit*," she remarked in a drawn out voice affected from the weed. TaTa sang along, while Shea listened intently to Nas's part, the way he spoke of Nicholas Barns.

Shea began to think about the rise and fall of some of the major hustlers from Harlem. Barnes, Kirkland, Rich, Po, and many more.

"Ta, you hear that shit? That's real, B. Gulliani ain't trying to see no black man turn into the next John Gotti! And Kane be actin' like an ole doofie ass bitch, spending money like this coke business is gonna last them forever."

"Oh boy, here we go again," TaTa joked. "Look Shea, I'm quite sure Kane know what she's doing. If she didn't have it to spend she wouldn't. Besides, she has always been good at saving up for a rainy day. And when you speak about her like that, you sound envious like or a little jealous."

Shea did have a lot of larceny in her heart for her sister, and no one ever understood why. Shea was just as pretty, her body didn't attract as much attention as Kisa's. Where she was skinny, Kisa was thicker. She didn't have a natural glow like Kisa. Where Kisa was a giver Shea was a taker. "Whatever, TaTa. You always take her side."

"You know what, Shea? I'm not even gonna argue with you. I know my cousin, and I know she gon' be okay. Besides, whenever you're in a bind she always manage to get your ass out. I surly don't hear you complaining when she loans you money that you never pay back. And when Cakey died, and his Mama came and took all the money and cars. Who came and gave you forty thousand to get back on your feet?"

"Fuck you, TaTa!"

With that Shea said no more as they exited onto 125th street.

As everyone walked into Kisa's Apartment, they smelled food.

Kisa told them, "I picked up some jogging suits, underwear, and Timbs for y'all. So y'all can eat and take showers before you leave."

TaTa warmed the food for everyone while Shea sat around with her lips poked out. She was still mad about the conversation she and TaTa had had in the car.

After everyone showered and got ready to eat, Sincere asked Kisa to run his bath water. Kisa cleaned the tub and ran his bath water while he ate with his niggas. She told him his bath was ready, and he asked his crew to stay for a short meeting.

Sincere walked into the bathroom. Kisa was laying out towels and underwear for him. She was getting ready to leave when Sincere asked her, "Can you stay in here with me? Matter of fact why don't you hop in the tub with me?"

"No, Sin, 'cause you know where it will lead, and we have company. We can do it all night after they leave."

"Well just help me wash and talk to me, okay?" Sincere asked with puppy eyes.

"Sure, bay, I'll do that for you."

"Damn, Kane, you always holding me down, fuck all them other hoes. That's why I wanna do it right."

Kisa rolled her eyes, "What are you talking about now, Sincere?"

"Ma, lets get married and do it the right way, a big wedding and everything. And I want to do it next month."

"Next month? Sincere, it takes longer than a month to plan a nice wedding."

"Well, we'll just have to try. Look, I go back to court in two months, and we don't know how this shit is going to turn out. Ma, we have to face the fact that I may have to do time."

"Come on, Sin, don't talk like that."

"Kisa, just say yes. Please?"

Kisa paused for a moment. "First you have to promise me that you will tell me everything even if you are worried about me being scared."

"Kane, what are you talking about?"

"Sincere I don't appreciate having to find out about your beef with Carlos from Shea. You know she rubbed it all in my face."

Sincere began to speak, but Kisa cut him off.

"You don't have to explain, just say you promise."

"I promise, baby."

"Well I guess I will marry you for real!"

Sincere pulled her in the water fully clothed in her new Fendi outfit and hugged her tight.

"Ma, I love you."

"I know, nigga. I love you too, but damn nigga did you have to pull me in the tub and fuck up my new clothes?"

"I'll buy you two more of these!"

"Speaking of buying, you know a last-minute wedding is going to be real expensive."

"So what? Spend what ever you need to. Anything for my lil' nigga."

"Well hurry up and finish, then you can get everybody out of here, so we can celebrate. There is some Cristal in the refrigerator, and I got a couple bags of Branson so we can get right."

Kisa got out of the tub and walked out the bathroom, soaking wet. Even though she didn't show it to Sincere, she was ecstatic at the thought of a real wedding.

Kisa walked into the bedroom. Shea and TaTa were lying across her bed. Shea couldn't let a moment of sarcasm pass. "Why are you wet and what's with that goofy ass smile on your face? I know y'all nasty asses wasn't in there doing it."

Kisa knew how Shea was so she lingered in the moment.

"No, bitch, we wasn't doing it, but we are having a big wedding next month!"

TaTa looked at Shea and told her, "Now pick your face up off the floor!"   She turned to Kisa. "Congratulations, but I know I better be in it!"

"Girl you know you are one of my maid of honors, and I would like for you to be one, Shea, and of course I have to call Eisani to let her know."

Shea gladly accepted the invitation. "Sure lil' sis and big congrats."

TaTa broke in, "Oh, and we have to call Tyeis too. We all are going help you plan the flyest wedding New York City has ever seen!"

Meanwhile, in the living room, Sincere met with his three lieutenants.

"First thing, we are going to have to lay low until the trial. So basically you're gonna have to let the lil' niggas under you take care of your street B.I. Our charges are conspiracy, so we know someone is talking. Let's find who it is." He rubbed his chin. "Mazetti said they are serious about trying to bring federal charges and using the RICO law. From here on out we'll just meet for dinner, you know, to make everything look kosher. We can't panic; we have to keep the business running smoothly. And of course, they already got me pegged for the ringleader, so I'll definitely be keeping a low profile. I'll just be spending most of my time with Kane planning our wedding."

"Your *what?*" Mannie barked out.

"My wedding, nigga, You heard me right the first time. And all of you will be in the wedding."

"That's what's up, my nigga," Butta said, giving Sincere a hug and a pound.

Shawn said, "Shit, ya niggas is already married by common law. What you need to have a wedding for?"

Sincere laughed, knowing his man didn't really understand.

"I just want to make it official and special for my baby. But her and me are about to pop some Cris and go half on a baby. Now, you ain't got to go home, but you got to get the hell out of here! Holla!"

Track 4: Remember the Good Times

The month had gone by so fast. It was already February the 14th, the wedding day. Kisa and Sincere had decided on an evening candlelight service. The church was dark barley illuminated by candles.

Kisa wore a winter-white, straight Vera Wang dress trimmed in white mink. Sincere had to fight back tears at the sight of her mother and father walking her down the aisle.

Kisa could not contain herself. Her man looked fabulous in his all black Armani Modern tux. Her bridesmaids wore beautiful, black, strapless, A-line dresses that draped the floor.

The church was packed with the who's who of the New York, the hustlin' world, and the hip-hop industry. And of course it wouldn't be a hustler's wedding if the feds and cops weren't there taking pictures.

The vows were short and sweet. Kisa surprised everyone when Faith serenaded Sincere with, *I'm So Glad You Came And Found Me* and *Give Me The Reasons To Love You* during the exchange of the rings.

Sincere knew his baby had good taste. His ring was platinum, but it looked like a never-ending circle of baguettes. The setting was completely hidden.

Kisa's new ring wasn't too shabby either; he gave her a ten-carat jacket to go around the five-karat engagement ring.

The reception was held at The Marriott, downtown Manhattan. Shrimp and lobster were served. Cristal was overflowing everywhere. The open bar was running out of liquor fast. Kisa danced the night away by herself or with anyone who would dance with her. Sincere had to pull her away at times.

All Kisa's girls were scoping out the room for ballers who were alone. When it was time to throw the bouquet, Kisa was so drunk, she could barely throw it. Without falling on her flat on her face.

The reception lasted till 3 a.m., or at least that's what time Kisa and Sincere went up to their suite and made love all night. But there was something different about this time. Out of the hundreds of times that Kisa and Sincere had had sex, neither had ever felt such a warm sensation. They looked directly in each other's eye and simultaneously said, "I love you."

The next day they were off to Italy for their honeymoon. Actually it was more than a honeymoon. Sincere brought Shawn, Mannie, and Butta, so Kisa brought Shea, TaTa, and Eisani.

Italy was beautiful. Kisa loved shopping and eating in the genuine Italian shops and restaurants. Sincere loved being in Italy. At night, when he and Kisa were alone, he'd tell her, "I love this country. The people here are loyal to one another. Men built great Mafia families here and really lived by a code of silence. I brought you here to see where my grandfather came from."

"I never knew you were mixed with Italian. I always thought you were half Spanish."

"Well my grandmother was his mistress, but he took care of us. He taught me the meaning of Omerta. That was the code he lived by. He is a made man and a good soldier." He threw his arm around Kisa's neck.

"Right now he is in the Metropolitan Detention Center serving his fifth year of a ten-year sentence for a bullshit charge that the feds hit him with just to get him to rat on higher ups. They came at him with all kinds of gimmicks, but he wouldn't take them. He stayed loyal to his family. And now they reward him."

"Sin why didn't you tell me before?"

"Kane, I don't tell anyone, but I've wanted to tell you for a while. My grandfather introduced me to my coke connect, who I'll be introducing you to!"

Kisa's face looked really uneasy. "No, Sin, I told you before; I want no parts of the business anymore."

"Look, ma, none of these niggas know my connect. If I have to go away, depending on how long, I want you to run things. You are the only person I completely trust with every aspect of my life besides my grandfather and Butta. All I need you to do is meet with the connect twice a month to pay him. The rest is set up for you. Your hands don't get dirty. You'll meet him tomorrow night at dinner."

"So your mind is just made up Sin. Without consulting me, huh?"

"Look, baby, I don't want to worry you but I am really fucked up by these charges. I can't beat all of them; so I'll most likely be away six months to a year. I need you to hold me down while I'm gone."

"Sin, you know I got you, but I thought Mazetti said since they found no drugs there would be no hard evidence?"

"That's what I thought too, but between the surveillance and the informant's testimony, he told me to expect some minimum time."

"And when were you going to let me know?"

"Know what?"

"Just fuck it Sin, I'm tired and I'm going to bed."

That night Kisa slept on the very end of the bed as Sincere lay awake unable to sleep. He rolled over and pulled Kisa close to him. She woke and tried to fight him off but he held her close and told her,

"I need you. Please, at least lay close to me."

He felt the tears drop on to his arm.

"I need you too Sin. I asked you to get out; you didn't. Now you're leaving me alone out here in the world."

She could hear Sincere begin to speak.

"No, Sin, please, don't say anything else. You'll only make it worse. I'll stay close. Just let me sleep, please."

The next morning everyone could feel the tension between Kisa and Sincere. Kisa stayed close to Eisani and TaTa, but she could not tell them what was going on.

Shea and Butta were in their own world, so Shea was too caught up in Butta to be concerned with what she called one of *Kisa's moments*.

That night, Kisa and Sincere had a private dinner in the home of Venicio Corletti, a good-looking Italian man in his late thirties. He was dark and his body was in splendid condition. Sincere told Corletti of a situation while Corletti's wife entertained Kisa in the next room. Kisa was having so much fun, she almost forgot that she and Sincere were beefing. Maria Corletti was only two years older than Kisa. She was sassy, gorgeous, and she was almost as dark as Kisa. She looked more West Indian than Italian. To top it off, she was fly.

She gave Kisa a dress, personally designed by Donatella Versace. She told Kisa in her beautiful accent, "I had this made especially for you. You will never see another one like it."

"Thank you. It is so beautiful."

"You are very welcome. I can take you to some private boutiques in the morning before you leave."

In the study, Corletti spoke like a father or older brother to Sincere. "Now, are you sure about letting a woman run your affairs? I mean I know she is your wife but what does she know about the business? Can she even run a business? I know you probably tell her everything, but that's another thing from actually being a part of it. Now when your grandfather asked me to help you, I assured him that I would help you make sound decisions and help you out when you were in a bad situation. And quite frankly, I still think Mazetti may be able to help you out."

Sincere sat back and took everything in that Corletti had to say before speaking. "I trust you and value your opinion very much. You've taken good care of me, I profit financially and mentally from this relationship. Now Kisa is the only person I trust to run the business, and not just because she is my wife. Kisa has already been involved in the game heavily. She's, no doubt, a very savvy businesswoman and handles herself better than a lot of the men I know. A year ago when I asked her to settle down with me, she expressed to me that she wanted to get out of the business. I told her as long as I'm around, she wouldn't have to hustle. Now, since I have to go away, the only way things will stay on track until I get back is if she handles it. She never talks to the jakes or the Feds, and she never discusses our business with anyone outside the family blood or business."

"Well, young Sincere, if you have no doubts, I have none either. I'll just have to take your word on this one. But let's just wait and see how everything turns out before we go jumping to conclusions. I won't be at the trial, but I'll be in the States keeping tabs on how everything's going. So if push comes to shove, I'll be prepared to meet with Mazetti and Kisa to set everything in motion. If that's everything lets break bread."

On the flight home, everyone talked and laughed about how much fun they'd had on the trip. There was still a noticeable difference in Kisa's attitude, and she slept during the flight.

Eisani made sure to grab Kisa when they got off the plane. "Kane, what's up wit my twin cousin?"

"Nothing, girl, just glad that flight is over."

"Nah, Kane, you been actin a little funny the last couple of days."

"E, baby, right now is not the time to talk about it."

"Well then you and I are going to the Shark Bar for dinner and drinks. "You can tell me the problem then, 'cause you are not even the same with Sincere and I am seriously worried about you. So I'll pick you up around seven. See you uptown."

"Yeah, whatever," Kisa mumbled as Eisani walked away.

Sincere and Kisa walked towards Butta's Escalade. "Kane, you still mad at me?"

"Sin, I told you I'm not mad; I just don't feel like being bothered."

"What do you mean, you don't feel like being bothered? I'm your fucking husband."

"Well act like it."

"What the fuck does that suppose to mean?"

"Just fuck off, Sincere."

At that instance Butta, Shawn, and Mannie knew it was pretty serious. They had never heard Kisa talk to Sincere like that. In fact, Kisa and Sincere had never gotten into it like this in front of anyone.

Mannie saw the way Sincere was glaring at Kisa and decided to step in. He knew by the look in

Sincere's eyes that he was about to grab his wife and choke the shit out of her. "Don't do it, dawg. You know she probably just suffering from PMS or something."

"Nah, Mannie, it ain't that. She just acting like a lil' bitch; like she new to the game. If she don't fix her face, I'm gonna smack the shit out of her ass."

"Yeah, whatever, Sincere. As a matter of fact I'll catch a cab home!"

"No, you will not. Get your ass in that truck Kisa."

"No! And fuck you Sincere. You don't have any considerations for my feelings, so don't worry about what I do! I'm out!"

Butta walked over to Sincere. "Fam, just let her go. Maybe she needs to be alone for a while."

Shawn added his two cents. "Come on man let's go to Sus Rendezvous; you been under Kane to long. I can't even remember the last time you hit something besides her."

"Nigga, watch it! That's still my wife! Anyway I need to work this one out now. Let's be out."

"Where you going Jersey, or uptown?" Butta asked Sincere.

"Take me uptown. That tech guy can't get over to Jersey until tomorrow to check the house for bugs. As a matter of fact take me downtown; I need to pick up some things."

To Kisa it seemed to be taking forever to get uptown. She knew the cab driver was trying to jerk her and take her the long way. She really didn't care though; she needed the time to think.

Kisa wasn't really mad at Sincere about putting her back in the game, because she would do anything for him. And she was honored that he trusted her enough to run his business.

The reality of the situation was he wasn't even gone and already she felt alone. She was a newlywed getting ready to be alone all over again. Kisa knew that blocking Sincere out would help her to adjust if he had to leave for prison. She really wanted to stop her act, but she was very stubborn by nature. She wasn't ready to go home and face Sincere.

She told the Cabdriver, "Yo, poppi, take me to 96th and Amsterdam."

Getting a manicure and pedicure was a sure-fire way to relax her. She stayed at the salon getting the works. She didn't get home until five hours later. When she walked through the door she was welcomed by the sounds of Faith.

She had not expected Sincere to be there, or maybe she expected for his entire crew to be there playing Play Station and smoking out. She passed by the bathroom and heard water running. She figured Sincere was on his way out.

On her bed laid two-dozen yellow roses, with a note that read, *Come on lil' mama, quit playing with me. One Love, your nigga.*

Kisa couldn't help but blush; she loved Sincere's sense of humor. Still she wasn't ready to give up her hard act. At the foot of the bed on the floor were a stack of gift bags from Gucci, Channel, and Fendi. Kisa wanted to ignore everything but she couldn't.

In the small Gucci gift bag she found three monogrammed bra and panty sets. The bigger Gucci gift bag contained a pair of knee-high black Gucci boots with a gold G hanging from the zippers, and a black lab coat to match. *He is really trying, but so far so good.*

In the Channel bag was a pair of oversized shades, logo stockings and a pair of black stilettos.

The Fendi bag was huge, so she knew it was something good. She pulled a heavy garment bag out of the gift bag.

"It can't be!" she said with a big grin. She unzipped the garment bag and sure enough, it was exactly what she thought it was. The Russian Fendi Sable full-length coat she had been dying for.

Sincere had known how bad Kisa wanted the coat. He even knew that she was saving for it. He also knew that this was a great way to get back on her good side.

When he was buying the coat he'd told himself, *This better work. For eighty thousand, it damn sure better work.*

Kisa was so excited, she completely missed the matching hat and the oversized Fendi tote bag.

Sincere came into the room five minutes later. He expected Kisa to be upset; he knew her to hold grudges for days. When he entered the room Kisa had the coat on, wearing nothing underneath. "I see you like your coat."

"Like it? I love it, baby. Thank you."

"I didn't think you would take to it so quickly I mean, seeing how mad you were earlier. And you know how you were iggin' me the last few days of the trip."

Kisa felt ashamed. She walked over to Sincere and gave him a big hug and kiss.

"Sin I know I've been a real bitch, and its not just about you putting me back in the game; I'm actually elated that you trust me that much. Baby, I just worry about loosing you every single day. I thought that if we were on bad terms when you left, it wouldn't hurt that much. I know that was very selfish of me. Then I look at you going through all this, and you're still worrying about my happiness. Thank you for the gifts. You didn't have to do all this. But it did make me forgive you a little quicker. Most of all, thanks for being a wonderful husband."

"Ma, I already knew what was wrong, and I knew I put a lot of pressure on you. I'm sorry about the way I got on you earlier, and I'm sorry you have to be going through all of this. But I do thank you for standing by me through everything; it ain't a lot of chicks that would stand by a nigga, especially all the shit with the other bitches. Kisa, I promise you in two years we will be strictly legit. Ma I just need to spend the next two weeks close to you, no beefing. So can we end this now?"

Kisa looked him in his eyes. "Say no more my Nigga." With that she gave him her Miss America smile.

Sincere looked at her for what seemed to be an eternity and said, "I love you, Mrs. Montega."

She replied, "I love you more, Mr. Montega."

"Then take that coat off and take a bath with me."

Kisa was taken aback when she saw the bathroom. The tub was filled with white rose pedals, and candles lit the room. Sincere came in behind her with two glasses and a bottle of Cristal. They sat in the tub and talked and laughed for over an hour.

The ringing of Kisa's cell phone ringing broke the monotony. She stood up to go get it; Sincere pulled her back down.

"Sit down. Just let it ring."

"Baby, I can't, that's Eisani. We had plans to go out."

"Well you better cancel them."

Kisa answered the phone, laughing, "Hello?"

"Well don't you sound like a million bucks," Eisani said.

"I feel like a billion, bitch," Kisa replied giggling, tipsy from the Cristal.

Eisani asked, "And why is that?"

"Sin and I are working on it now."

"I bet y'all are."

"Well then you know the Shark Bar is over for me!"

"I know, girl, I'm just happy to know you're feeling better. Why don't we have lunch tomorrow and you can tell me all about it."

"Sounds great, and we can go downtown so I can get some pantsuits to wear to the trial."

"That sounds good. I'm Staying in the Bronx tonight, so I'll pick you up on my way downtown. Alright, Ma, I love you."

"Love you too E. One."

Kisa was standing in the middle of the bedroom naked and dripping wet. Sincere walked up behind her and began kissing her all over her neck and back. He bent her forward over the bed and slid inside of her. After a few strokes, he pulled out slowly and ran his tongue over her warm vagina. That made Kisa's entire body go limp.

He turned her over and attempted to get on top, but she pushed him backwards and mounted him. As Kisa rode him she felt slight twinges of pain in her abdomen. She kept going anyway. A minute later the pain was too overwhelming; she pulled her body off of Sincere's and balled over in pain.

At first Sincere thought she was having an orgasm, until she spoke. He could hear the pain in her voice and see it in her face.

"Sin, it hurts so bad."

"What's hurting you, baby?"

"My stomach!"

"What does it feel like?"

"I don't know," Kisa cried.

"Come on, let's get dressed, I'm taking you to the hospital."

"No, it's probably just my period coming. Can you hand me some PJ's and let me lay down for a while?"

"Are you sure, Ma?"

"I'm positive, and when it passes I'll give you some slow neck."

Sincere laughed. "Let me find out you having my seed, and you not telling me."

"Whatever, nigga."

"I'm gonna make you some tea, and I'll bring the DVD player in here so we can watch some movies."

Kisa thought to herself, *I love that nigga.*

The next morning, Kisa was awakened by the ringing phone, which was sitting right next to her head. "Hello?" She halfway yelled into the phone.

"Kane, I know you not still sleeping!"

"Eisani? What time is it?"

"It is eleven o'clock. Get ya ass out that bed."

Kisa sat up and looked around, noticing Sincere's absence. As long as they had been together, he never left without waking her.

Eisani interrupted Kisa's train of thought. "I'm on my way to you now, so throw on something and be Ready!"

"What's the dress code for today?"

"Jeans and Sneakers."

"I'll be ready in thirty minutes; just call me when you're outside. One."

"One."

Kisa showered and dressed for a nonstop shopping day. She put on her favorite jeans, a black sweater, black Prada sneakers, and a black Prada bomber jacket with the matching bag and baseball cap. The intercom rang.

"Who?"

"Eisani. Let me up."

"I'm ready to come down."

"No, I need to come up and use the bathroom."

Kisa buzzed her in and waited by the door. When the elevator opened Eisani came running out full speed.

Kisa saw her coming and stepped out of the way.

"Damn, E, you got a bladder infection or something?"

"Shut up and don't shut the door; Sincere and Mannie was behind me." Eisani yelled as she rushed to the toilet.

Kisa turned around and was face to face with Sincere. "Hi baby."

He grabbed her and hugged her tight.

Mannie walked past them, joking, "I'm glad to see Bonnie and Clyde are getting along."

Kisa pulled out of Sincere's grasp, smelling the scent of weed. He never smoked this early in the day, or outside his home. She looked at his eyes; they were red-shot from the weed. "Why didn't you wake me this morning?"

"It was early and I didn't want to bother you after you wasn't feeling good last night."

"Well, sweetie, where did you go?"

"I just went for a ride, you know. I needed to clear my head."

This time she looked into his eyes and saw that they were filled with worry. "Baby are you okay you seem sad."

"Kane everything is okay. Ma stop worrying."

Eisani emerged from the back, excited. "Bitch when did you get that Fendi Sable?"

"My baby gave it to me last night,"

Kisa answered, smiling ear-to-ear, holding Sincere by the waist.

"Come on, ma, let's be out. I'll tell you all about it."

She kissed Sincere goodbye. As she walked out the door, she turned and looked at him one more time. She felt so sad for him she wanted to break down and cry.

For Kisa and Eisani it was a comfortable fun day. They walked all over the city shopping. They actually did more window-shopping. They parked in midtown and caught the train to the Village. It had been years since either of them had rode the train.

They were having so much fun bugging out on the train. They rode it all the way uptown to their favorite Italian restaurant Presto's for lunch. After lunch, they returned to midtown to be pampered at the spa. On the way into the salon, Eisani got a phone call from Elijah.

Kisa went ahead inside and signed their names. Twenty minutes later Eisani joined Kisa in the waiting area, and she was visibly upset.

Kisa could tell that Eisani had been crying. "Eisani, what's wrong?"

"Nothing, just fucking Elijah."

She dropped her head in her hands and let out a little whimper.

Kisa had never seen Eisani cry over a guy. She slid close and put her arms around Eisani. "E tell me what happened? What did he say?"

At that moment two salon attendants came out to get them. Kisa looked over at Eisani. "Do you want to leave, Ma?"

"No, we can stay. I need this. I will talk to you in the sauna."

They went their separate ways. They both got the works: full body waxes, massages, and mud baths. During Eisani's treatment, all she could think about was her deteriorating relationship with Elijah. In another room, all Kisa could think about was seeing Eisani cry over Elijah.

Kisa walked into the sauna and sat directly in front of Eisani. She turned around to face her. "E, are you ready to talk now?"

Eisani took a deep breath. "Kane, you know how I am about guys. I would rather be by myself than go through all the bullshit. But when I met Elijah he caught me off guard. He was all man. I thought he was the one I had been waiting for. You know I thought he was the one I was destined to be with. I thought he would be the one to take me out the streets. I mean, I knew he was coming out of a rocky relationship, and at first it seemed like we were past that. Then come to find out the chick is about to have his baby and I guess now they're trying to work it out or something. After I put my heart and time into it, he is still going through the motions with her again. Then he tells me how much he needs me, and to just bear with him until he gets through the situation. And some days I feel like he's running game on me, but he is so sincere about everything. Kane, I'm feeling him. I might even love him, I'm so confused I don't know what to do."

Again Eisani began to cry. Seeing her like this made Kisa sad. She didn't know what to say or how to start. She was so used to Eisani being her strength that it took her a few minutes to get her words together. "E, now you know I'm not the best person when it comes to love advice. Just look at all the shit I've been through with Sincere, but that's a relationship, baby. And relationships take a lot of work. There are going to be days that are filled with hurt and heartache. You have to ask yourself, do the good days outweigh the bad? I remember after I left CoCo, for a long time I would question my decision. I asked myself often, did I give up on him too soon? Should I have at least tried to work it out?' I don't question it now but I learned from it. So I was prepared with Sincere. Now, I'm not saying take unnecessary shit from him. But if you're feeling him like you say you do, try and work it out. But stop beating yourself up, alright."

"Alright."

"And if he give you anymore problems, you know I will come through and do my thug thizzle, ma," Kisa said causing Eisani to crack a smile.

"Kane, you are still as silly as you were when we were little. But thanks. I needed to laugh."

"Ma, it's nothing. Come on, let's be out."

Eisani let Kisa out in front of her building. She drug herself upstairs with five shopping bags in each hand. She was tired and her feet were finally giving out on her. When she got outside of her door, she heard loud talking and music. She thought to herself, *Not tonight.*

When she opened the door a cloud of weed smoke hit her. She dropped her bags and walked towards the living room. It was filled with Sincere's regular crew plus three of his younger cousins. They were so loud they didn't even notice her standing there.

The Play Station NBA tournament was in full effect. There was almost five thousand dollars in bet money lying on the table. Heineken bottles were everywhere; Shawn and Mannie were busy arguing about who had the best CD out. Kisa stopped the music, causing everyone to jump until they saw who it was. They all greeted her at once. "What up, Kane?"

"What up, y'all?"

Sincere paused the game and followed her into the bedroom. He came up behind her and hugged her.

"How was your day?"

"My day was wonderful."

"I bet it was I saw all those bags by the door."

"Nah, it wasn't just the shopping; it was really fun. We hung out, shopped, talked, did the spa thing, and we even rode the train."

"Wait a minute. You rode the train?"

"Yes, I did! And what did you do today? Besides smoke up the apartment."

"I just hung out here all day I missed you."

Kisa sat next to Sincere on the dresser.

"I missed you too, and I was worried about you."

"Why were you worried?"

"You seem so zoned out. Leaving the house without speaking and the early morning smoking... Is there anything you want to talk about?"

He rubbed her thigh. "Its nothing, ma I'm just trying to relax, you know, and get my mind off the trial. So you can stop worrying your little pretty self." He kissed her on the forehead and hopped off the dresser.

Kisa decided not to press the issue anymore. "Well, what do you want for dinner?"

"We just ordered pizza."

Kisa was so relieved. "That's straight, 'cause I am so tired."

"Oh yeah! We can move back in the townhouse this week. The furniture will be delivered after two tomorrow."

"How much did the house repairs run you altogether?"

"With the paint, it ran a little over fifteen g's. I know if I beat trial, I should sue them jakes for fucking up the house and the cars."

"Baby, if you beat trial, I want you to stay as far away from those jakes as you can!"

They fell out laughing. Sincere knew he was going away; he just didn't know how long. He was worried sick, but he couldn't let Kisa see it. As they sat and joked, he laughed hard to keep from crying. It was little stolen moments like this that he would miss the most.

He stopped laughing and stared at her. When she realized he had stopped, she traded stare with his glassy eyes and asked, "Baby this is my last time asking, are you being straight with me?"

"Kisa I'm always straight with you."

He kissed her again. "Now go ahead and get some rest, 'cause you know when they leave its going to be on and poppin. And you still owe me from last night." Sincere left the room happy he hadn't cracked under Kisa's questioning. Especially when she looked at him with those big brown eyes.

Kisa stretched out across the bed and tried to analyze the situation. But as soon as her head hit the pillow she was out.

The next two weeks flew by so quickly. Kisa couldn't believe it was already the first day of Sincere's trial. Court was just how she'd seen it in the movies. The bailiff walked in and announced, "All rise for the Honorable Jonathan Weinstein. Case 1224, the State of New York vs. Sincere Christopher Montega, NaShawn Rafik Hudson, Manuel Angel Santana, and Carlos Antonio Santee. The charges are conspiracy to traffic and distribute a controlled substance, and possession of illegal firearms."

The prosecutor wasted no time getting to the point. He had witness after witness testifying about deals they had made with Sincere. Most of the witnesses Sincere had never seen a day in his life. Mazetti won most of his objections based on evidence or hearsay rules. He also slayed all of the prosecutor's witnesses on cross-examination.

By the fourth day of trial, it seemed like the state's case was dwindling right before their eyes. That is, until the state called, Maurice Jones, a former worker of the crew. He had been fired because he could not keep his nose out of the cocaine, and his hand from skimming money off the top.

He had a strong dislike for Sincere. He had even thought about murdering him. When Mannie brought it to Sincere's attention, about Maurice's sticky fingers, they beat him so bad he almost died. Sincere wanted him to live. The scars were a living testimony to everyone of what would happen if you crossed Sincere.

Ever since that day, Maurice swore his revenge and he felt this was the safest way. The state promised him money and a new identity in exchange for his testimony. Maurice had not worked for Sincere in over two years; his testimony didn't corroborate the Street Sweepers' surveillance.

Kisa could tell that the jury was moved by his testimony about his long recovery and the effect it had on his family. She wanted to stand up and yell out, "You know your whole family is a bunch of drunks and crackheads; they don't give a fuck about your trifling ass." She managed to hold her composure.

Mazetti tried to break Maurice on cross-examination, but he wouldn't budge. He stuck to his exact testimony. The best Mazetti did was to get him to admit that he accepted money from the state in exchange for his testimony, and immunity for any of his existing state charges.

The defense's case was short, only lasting two days, and mostly calling character witnesses to tear down the monstrous picture the state had painted of Sincere and his codefendants.

While the jury was out deliberating, Kisa, Sincere, Mannie, Butta, Shawn, and Eisani went to Houlahans for lunch. They all ate in silence. All of a sudden Sincere began breaking. "I swear I'm gon' merk that nigga Maurice. Fucking faggot! I should have killed him back then."

Mannie looked at Sincere and told him, "Fam, don't even worry. As soon as he settles down in his new location, somebody gon' put two in his rat mouth."

Kisa interrupted, "Come on now. Y'all talking reckless and shit and as a matter of fact lets get back to the courthouse. The jury might be back soon."

Two hours after the jury came back from lunch, they returned with a verdict. Kisa entered the courtroom just in time. She sat next to Sincere's mother, Lena on the bench directly behind the defendants where she had been permanently for the last two weeks.

The codefendants and their lawyers entered the courtroom. A few minutes later, the bailiff announced, "All rise for the Honorable Judge Weinstein."

The judge took his seat at the bench. "Please bring the jury in now." The jury filed into the courtroom slowly. The bailiff retrieved a piece of paper from the jury foreman. Judge Weinstein read the paper and sent it back to the foreman. The foreman stood up. The judge asked him, "In the case of the state of New York vs. Sincere Christopher Montega. Count one, Operating a criminal enterprise. What is your verdict?"

"We find the defendant not guilty your honor."

"Count two, conspiracy to traffic and distribute a controlled substance. What is your verdict?"

"We find the defendant not guilty your honor."

Sincere began to feel a great since of relief come over him.

The judge continued to get the verdicts, for each defendant. Although Sincere and his codefendants had been found not guilty for each narcotics violation, the jurors found it necessary to stick them with the illegal firearms possession.

"The defendants are to be held in the custody of the state of New York corrections until sentencing one week from today." The judge dismissed the jury and banged his gavel. That was the end of the trial.

Kisa and Mazetti were allowed a few minutes with Sincere. Kisa wanted to break down and cry, but she and Sincere had been through this a thousand times over the past week.

When Sincere finished talking to Mazetti, he saw the squinted up look on Kisa's face.

"Ma, please don't cry I can't go in there with my head straight if you're crying when I walk away."

"But, baby, I never really got it through my head that I would be going home without you. Sin, what am I gonna to do out here in the world without you?"

"When you think of me, just remember the good times."

Track 5: When the Money Get Low

Kisa missed Sincere dearly. He had been sentenced to fifteen months on the island. It had only been three weeks since the sentencing hearing. Kisa cried the first night. After that she cleared her head and it was full speed ahead.

She'd already had her first meeting with Corletti. Corletti sold the kilos to Sincere for five thousand dollars whenever he bought twenty or more. Kisa now knew why he didn't want anyone else handling this connect. With kilos going at $20,500 during plus a lot more during a drought, not to mention the broken down weight that Sincere was putting on the street, his profit was almost damn near one hundred percent.

Kisa made a note to herself to check the percentages after the first month's profits came in. Her first deal with Corletti was $200,000 for forty Ki's. Kisa's new role was exhausting. She had to make sure the coke was picked up, and make sure everyone got what they were suppose to all over NY.

After the first day she knew she had to put her own team together. She quickly divided the duties between Shea, TaTa, Eisani, and herself. The first day, Kisa had to pick up money. She did not get home until 4 a.m. Now she understood why Sincere was away so much. She promised herself she would never fight with him again about being gone two days straight. And she still had to run the paper through the money counter machine. She was more fatigued than usual. After picking up the money she had to give half to Mazetti to be deposited in an overseas account, then she would have to do payroll.

Kisa was driving across the George Washington Bridge when she remembered she had not had a period since before the wedding. As soon as she got off in the city, she went to Duane Reade and bought three EPT tests.

She was going to take the test at the salon but decided against it. When Kisa walked into the salon, all the chickens were in there clucking. "Hi, Kane," they sang out.

Kisa gave them a half "hi." She knew these were the same bitches spreading rumors about her being back in the 'hood because Sincere was in jail and had left her broke. Kisa was glad about that rumor, though; it would keep the heat off of her for a while. She knew that the Street Sweepers were bragging that they had shut down Sincere's operation.

Kisa had to pick up the last of the money from her workers on the street. First she had to take this money to Eisani, in the back office, and let her run it through the money counter.

When Kisa walked into the office, she saw Eisani totaling the books. "Hi E., what's poppin'?"

"Nothing cousin. Finishing the books."

"Here is the money I picked up from the Eastside. Count that for me so I can go pick up the last of this paper from them young boys in the Bronx."

"Yo, Kane, you made a killin' this week. I know we made about $800,000 before paying everybody."

"Sin said it was only like that because we had to make up the loss for the month."

"Yeah, that's right; I forgot about that," Eisani replied.

"Yo, E, I'm hungrier than a hostage."

"Me too Ma I need some grub I didn't eat shit this morning."

"Well we can go to Ahirahs on Lenox"

"That's what's up."

There was a knock at the door.

Kisa and Eisani looked at each other; Kisa's heart dropped. "Who?"

"It's Tyeis nigga. Buzz me in"

"Oh, girl, don't be scaring me like that, chick. Eisani, buzz the door."

They watched their little cousin walk through the door. She was only seventeen but her body was already bananas. Tyeis could do the best weave uptown, so she was young and had paper. Tyeis had been through some major shit at an early age. When she was eight, her father beat her mother to death, Tyeis tried to save her but it was too late.   Tyeis grabbed her father's gat and blew him away. So Kisa always went easy on her younger cousin, even took her under the wing as a little sister. She put Tyeis through beauty school, helped her get an apartment and gave her furniture. But Tyeis was good. She held her own down.   She didn't need no nigga; everything she had she bought for her herself, something Kisa instilled in her.

"What up, Ty?" Kisa asked.

"Nothin', I'm chillin'.   You know same shit, different day."

"Shit, girl, you doing everybody hair in New York, what could be better!"

"Shit!" Eisani said, "You seventeen, bringing in four thousand dollars a week legally.   I know you better be saving."

Kisa answered that question for Tyeis. "Don't worry about that, I helped little mama open a bank account.   She good. How many heads you got out there?"

"Nigga, I'm through.   I was only working half a day today."

"Well, we going to eat in about fifteen minutes, when Eisani get through. Go clean your station and roll wit ya fam. After we eat and I finish all the pick-ups and drop-offs we can go shopping."

"I'm with it, Ma. I'll be ready when ya'll come out."

Kisa was now six months pregnant. The entire operation was running smoothly. It was summertime; Kisa was back in the 'hood for real. She could be seen quite often on Eighth Ave., hanging out with her cousins. She had actually doubled all of Sincere's profits, and he was proud of her. But he told her to be careful. She'd opened the business to too many new customers.

Sincere was happy about the thought of a first child but sad that he wouldn't be there for the birth. He was happy about his first child but sad that he wouldn't be there for the birth. Sin often tossed and turned from nightmares about Kisa being pregnant out in the world alone. His dream always started Kisa walking down Eighth Ave, belly swollen, skin glowing, and hair flowing. Then out of nowhere, renegade niggas just snatching her off the street and holding her for Ransom, not feeding her, beating her, and raping her.

After the nightmares started, Sincere doubled his daily calls. He knew that everyone knew she was back in the hood, and that she was running things. He was always hearing talk on the Island about a bitch that had shit on lock back in the world. So he knew that if everyone inside was talking, the streets were most definitely talking.

Since Kisa had opened the business up to new associates, her work was doubled, but the pregnancy slowed her down entirely. TaTa, Eisani, and Shea had now moved into the townhouse with her. Kisa was always tired, so she wasn't on point or focused with her duties. She started slipping not paying attention to her surroundings.

On a normal day she could spot grimy niggas plotting on her. The streets were paying plenty of attention to Kisa. Kisa and Eisani were in the back offices of the salon talking and counting the money, while Tyeis cleaned the shop.

Kisa was so tired, she had decided on taking the money out of the safe and just taking it home so she could sleep late and just take it to the drop off spot the next day.

"Eisani, what's your total?"

"I have $345,000. We'll put this last hundred thousand with it. I took out fifty g's to take all the workers."

"Just put all that in the Louis Vuitton knapsack and let's be out." Kisa opened the door. "Yo Ty, you ready? Do y'all want me to take y'all over to the garage to pick up your cars? Cause I was thinking I could leave my car in the garage and ride home with one of you. I swear I can't even get behind the wheel tonight."

Eisani replied, "You do look like shit, ma. So I'll leave my car here, and I can drive yours to Jersey."

Then Tyies said, "We don't even have to go to the garage. Just leave my car here and we can all ride together. I can spend the night with you all."

Tyeis attempted to set the alarm. "Kane, you need to call the alarm company again. This bum ass key-pad still has a short in it."

Kisa was too exhausted to worry about the alarm. "Forget all that. Just pull the gate down tonight and let's go."

They left the shop, laughing and joking as they climbed into the Range. Kisa looked back. No one was there, but she felt someone. As Eisani made the right onto Eighth Ave., from 125th street, Kisa felt the baby begin to kick rapidly. She liked the feeling of the baby moving around inside of her.

She smiled at the thought of life inside of her, blocking out Eisani and Tyeis' conversation. As Eisani approached 155th and Eighth, a black Land Cruiser cut them off, missing them by inches.

"What the fuck!" Kisa yelled, snapping out of her trance.

Suddenly there was a bang from the back. Eisani threw the truck in park. When Kisa turned to get out, glass shattered in her face. The next thing she felt was the end of a cold berretta against her temple.

A familiar voice rang out, but none of them could put their finger on it.

"Aight, everybody, put ya hands where I can see them. Do something stupid and I'm gonna leave your brains on the dash." The gunman spoke with a heavy Spanish accent.

Kisa thought to herself, *Of all the days to leave the secret compartment, I chose today.*

She attempted to look over at Eisani to see if she could gat in reach her own .22, but Eisani had a gun pointed at her face and so did Tyeis.

At once, all the doors of the Range Rover were yanked open and the three women were snatched out. One gunman smacked Kisa so hard, she fell back, but before she could hit the ground, he caught her by the collar and got real close to her face. "Bitch, we can do this the easy way or the hard way! You choose! Now hand over that paper or I'll start merking you hoes one by one. Starting with your pride and joy, little Miss Tyeis."

Kisa wasn't stupid. If she hadn't been pregnant and had her gat right on her, she might fight back. She knew the money could be replaced, and even if it couldn't, it wasn't more important than the child she carried, her cousins, or her own life. As she began to speak she could taste the salty blood in her mouth. "The money is in the Louis Vuitton knapsack in the back seat."

The gunman yelled for one of his henchmen. "Yo, lil' man, reach back there and grab that knapsack. Open it, nigga. Hurry the fuck up."

"Holy mother of Christ!"

"What's wrong?" The gunman asked, holding the gun steady between Kisa's eyes.

"Nigga, fuck that; ask me what's right. Look at all this fucking paper. It must be at least a quarter of a million dollars in here. She never said it would be anything like this, shit we hit the lotto this time."

The gunman looked into Kisa's eyes; his eyes were so insane and jumping around all wild.

Kisa promised that she would never forget them.

"You know what, bitch? I'm so happy I'm gonna let you live. But I am gon' whip your little pretty ass first."

Kisa felt a blow to the right side of her face then to the left. She could tell the cold piercing pains were from the gun. The third strike sent her tumbling to her knees. The gunman kicked her in the face with his steel-toed Timberland, and sent her straight on her back.

Tyeis and Eisani looked on, frozen by the chrome stuck next to their own heads, with tears streaming down their faces. They were helpless. The gunman bent down over Kisa.

"Now where your bitch-ass husband? Tell him I said pay back is a bitch, ain't it, and next time I will kill his bitch and that bastard ass baby."

Kisa was so disoriented, and her eyes were swelling fast.

She looked at him chillingly and said, "There won't be a next time!" She grabbed his face and kissed his forehead so hard it hurt.

Once he was out of Kisa's grasp he gave her a long hard stare and contemplated killing her, but he knew he would never get away with it. So he squashed it, even though he knew she had given him the kiss of death.

The sound of the sirens broke his trance. One of his boys yelled out, "Come on, nigga, the jakes is coming."

He looked down at Kisa. "Fuck you, you crazy bitch!" He spat on her, ran to the truck, and merked off.

Eisani immediately ran over to Kisa. "Oh my God, Kisa, baby, hold on. Ty, help me get her into the truck. We can take her to Harlem Hospital."

They laid Kisa in the back seat; Ty held Kisa's head in her lap. She wept and rubbed Kisa's hair softly. Eisani hit the U-turn so hard she almost turned the Range over. She headed toward 135th Street, sometimes reaching eighty miles per hour. Some of the cops responding to the robbery call turned to pursue the speeding Range Rover. Eisani led the cops right up to the Emergency room door.

As Eisani got out of the car, the cops yelled her, "Freeze! Police!"

She looked towards them and yelled, "Fuck that. You trigger happy fuckas just gonna have to shoot me but I'm gonna get my cousin into that hospital now!"

Another police car pulled up. The officer jumped out screaming, "Wait! Those are the victims."

Tyeis looked at them coldly. "I'm glad you figured that shit out. Now can we get some help?"

The police lifted a semi conscious Kisa out of the backseat, took her inside, and placed her on a stretcher.

Eisani explained to the doctors and the police what exactly her cousin had just went through. All Tyeis could do was cry and ask if Kisa would lose the baby. All the doctor would say was that he didn't know, and that he would fight hard for Kisa and the baby.

The doctor came back one hour later.

"Kisa and the baby are going to be fine," he told Eisani. "Your cousin is very strong. There was no harm to the uterus and abdominal area. Her face took a good beating. There were some slight fractures that will heal in no time along with the bruises. And her CAT scan showed no damage. But I'm going to keep her overnight for observation."

Tyeis asked, "Can we see her now?"

"Sure, go ahead."

"Thank you, sir. Come on, E."

Eisani and Tyeis entered the room and were disturbed over Kisa's face. They both were glad she was sleeping. They would not have wanted her to see their reactions. The dark, purple and blue bruises against her reddish brown skin were so awful. And the swelling around her eyes were twice the size they were when they brought her in.

To them her face looked so bad, it was hard to imagine her beauty ever returning. Tyeis and Eisani fell asleep in the chairs next to the bed.

The next morning they were awakened by the sound of Kisa's voice crying out for Sincere.

"Kisa, ma, wake up; you're having a nightmare," Eisani said as she gently shook her.

When Kisa woke up. She felt like she'd been kicked in the face. Someone had, but now the pain had intensified. Kisa looked at her cousins and began to cry.

"Please don't cry," Tyeis told her as she rubbed her hair.

"I'm glad y'all are here, but I need Sin, I need him now."

Eisani did what she could to comfort her cousin. "Ma, you know he's locked up. Ty, go get the doctor. Kisa I have the phone right here so you won't miss his call."

"E, have you talked to Shea? Why isn't she here yet? I need to get back to business... Get all this shit in order."

"No, you need to rest so you can heal," Eisani demanded.

"Look, E, I'm fine. But you have to realize I just got hit for half a mill. Plus I need to find out who is behind this. That voice sounded so familiar .It won't be too hard to find out though. Somebody gonna be spreading the love or yapping." Kisa tried to sit up straight feeling the need to get her point across.

"Look, niggas get shot six to ten times and walk out the hospital and carry on like its nothing. And carry on with business. My most important concern is the child inside of me, the doctor said the baby is fine. Sin won't be home for nine months; he trusted his business in my hands so I have to keep it moving. Only thing wrong with me is my face is fucked up to the fifth power, and my bank is light five hundred g's. So in order to solidify myself in this game, I have to get just as grimy as these niggas and play even uglier.

Once I talk to Sin and get my mind right, its definitely back to B.I."

At that moment, Shea and TaTa entered the room, followed by two detectives. Shea hugged her sister and kissed her face. As they embraced, a strange feeling came down over Kisa. After TaTa gave her sympathies, the DT's interrupted.

"Mrs. Montega, I'm Detective O'Neal, and this is Detective Santaval. How are you feeling?"

"I'm as well as can be expected."

"Well I only have a few questions for you. Do you know who your attackers were?"

"No, they wore masks."

"Do you know what their motive was?"

"Robbery, I guess, I mean they stole about fifteen hundred dollars that I had just collected from my salon, a ring, and bracelet I was wearing."

Eisani and Tyeis wanted to roll with laughter as they watched their cousin put on an Oscar-worthy performance, though she was banged up.

Detective Santaval set in on Kisa. "Mrs. Montega, we understand your husband is serving time on Rikers Island, and before going in he was involved in a heavy cocaine operation here in Harlem. Do you think this may be some type of retaliation towards him?"

"Not to my recollection," Kisa answered.

"What's not to your recollection? The fact that your husband is a petty gangster, or why you got robbed?" He asked with a smirk on his face.

Kisa spoke calm but firm.

"Get the fuck out! This questioning is over. If you want to speak to me again, call my lawyer."

Detective O'Neal interrupted. "Sorry about my partner's overzealous behavior. Here is my card. If any of you remember anything, don't hesitate to give me a call."

He handed everyone a card and followed his partner out of the room.

"Can you believe them assholes with that good-cop-bad-cop shit?" Kisa hissed.

"Don't even sweat that shit." Shea commented.

"I ain't sweating shit. And where the fuck y'all been? Never mind, I don't even want to know. Can y'all take Tyeis to Esplanade to get me some clothes while I get checked out?"

"Sure," TaTa said. "Do you want some food or something?"

"Nah, I'm straight. Just please be quick."

Kisa waited until she heard their footsteps drift down the hallway. Eisani studied her cousin's swollen eyes. "What's up, Kane? I see it all in your face."

"Yo, E, something is up with Shea, I could feel it all in her hug and in her presence."

"Now, Kisa I know you not trying to say you think your own sister had something to do with it."

Kisa took a deep breath. "All I'm saying is I know a girl set us up! You heard that nigga when he said, 'she never said it would be like this.' Who else knew how the operation ran besides her and TaTa? I know TaTa didn't have shit to do with it. Ta don't get down like that. And if she did, she don't fuck with blood family like that. Now Shea, this is her type of shit. She inherited that grimy shit from her mother's side. They all grimy as hell."

"You give everything to her; why would she go and do some fucked up shit like that?"

"That's it, the jealousy, which everyone knows about. And I'm her younger sister, and I support her. Plus Butta told Sincere how she was talking all greasy and reckless about us. I know she is my sister, but she is very malicious and cold hearted. And you can't forget when she set that nigga up, Black, from 149th and Amsterdam. Sincere had to get her stupid ass out that shit 'cause that nigga was gonna kill her simple ass. After all that, come to find out that's how she was making her extra money-setting niggas up."

"Well, Kane, what do you wanna do?" Eisani asked.

Kisa paused before answering. "I don't want to rush to judgment and fuck shit up, I'm just gonna keep her close and watch her. Also we're going to change the operation. Only the two of us and TaTa will know how it works. I'm not going to tell Sin until I'm sure, 'cause he'll have her wig split. Shit I'm going to kill that bitch if I find out."

"If that's how you want it, then that's how it's going down."

Once Kisa settled down in her own bed the phone rang.

"Hello?"

"Hey, baby girl."

"Hi, Sin. How are you, baby?"

"How are you and the baby doing?"

"Sincere, I have to talk to you. Please don't get all mad and angry?"

"Kisa, what's wrong? Is the baby okay?"

"The baby is great, but I was set up and robbed last night."

"By who?"

"I don't know. They wore masks and they got away with-"

Sincere interrupted, "Baby, I'm so sorry this shit is all my fault. You can tell me the other part when you come see me. Tell me did they do anything to you?"

"Sin, I don't want to upset you sweetie."

"No, Kisa, you have to tell me I need to know."

Kisa began to cry.   "Sin he beat me the face with a gun."

"With a gun!"

"Yeah, he fucked my face up bad, baby, and he told me to tell you 'payback's a bitch, ain't it'."

Sincere took a deep breath.

"Did you go to the hospital?"

"Yes, I spent the night I just got home."

"Ma, I'm so sorry.   Who was with you?"

"Eisani and Tyeis."

Sincere got heated all over again.   "I swear to God I'm gonna murder them niggas!   Baby, I love you. I am so sorry.   Please say you forgive me?"

"Bay it's not your fault; I was just caught slippin'."

"Kisa, when I hang up, I'm gonna call Big Terry and set up security for you. I know you don't like it but it has to be this way until I come home. I can't lose you, ma, especially while I'm locked up in here.   I would die. We can talk about everything when you come on Saturday."

"Sin, I don't think I should come this week. I don't want you to see me looking like this."

"Kisa, I don't give a fuck about those bruises, I know how you look. I need to see you."

Kisa gave in.   "Okay bay, I'll be there."

"Well let me call this nigga and get your security together, and I'll call you back. I love you baby."

"I love you too, Sin."

When Sincere hung up the phone, he nearly choked fighting back the tears. He knew his wife was tough, but he knew she was really hurting on the inside. And it was all his fault. After he swallowed it up, he called Terry and set up security for Kisa.

Once he finished his conversation, he met with Mannie, Shawn, and Butta. He swallowed hard before he began to speak.

"Kisa got robbed last night, and she said they fucked her face up. They beat her with a gun. I don't know how much they hit her for; she said we took a killing. I'm only worried about her and my seed. I don't want to discuss anything right now. I'm too heated. I just want y'all niggas to keep your ears open and find out who did this. I'm out."

Sincere walked away leaving everyone stunned. Mannie waited until Sincere was out of sight before he started talking. "Yo, I know, my nigga is hurting bad."

Butta shook his head. "I know he looked like he had been crying."

"Shit!" Shawn broke in. "You know that nigga was crying. Kisa is his heart. Whoever did this is going to die."

"I know." Butta replied. "If they don't want to die the better get ghost quick."

By the end of the day it was all over Harlem. Everyone knew about the heist. And it was the foolish niggas that did it, running their mouths about the great lick they had just hit. By Friday it was all over the island, and Sincere had a name-a name that hit too close to home.

When Sincere saw Kisa the next day, he regretted that he had begged her to come. The sight of Kisa's face made him even angrier. Everyone in the visitation was staring at her, not to mention she was six and a half months. She wore a white linen short set with white and black Chanel sneakers. Mannie and Butta could not believe how bad Kisa's face was; they knew Sincere had to be furious.

Sincere didn't speak for five minutes; he just rubbed and kissed her face. Eisani had accompanied Kisa. She told Mannie and Butta, "Let's go sit somewhere else. Let them be alone."

Sincere finally spoke. "I can't say enough how sorry I am."

Kisa interrupted him. "Bay I know already. Let's not get all mushy in here. Besides I'm all cried out."

"Okay, ma. I'm just so heated about your face. Put your shades back on so these fuckers will stop staring."

Kisa covered her eyes with the Chanel shades that Sincere had given her before he went in.

"Kane, I got the name of the person behind this."

"Who?"

"Cuban Joe, Shea's Cuban Joe."

He looked at her face, trying to read the expression. "Why don't you look surprised?"

Kisa shifted her pregnant body around in the chair. "I wasn't going to tell you this until I was sure. I felt Shea had something to do with this but I didn't want to tell you until I was sure."

"What?"

"One of the stick up kids made a comment, saying the girl never said the take would be that much. Plus I recognized Cuban's; voice I just couldn't place it. I'm going to kill that bitch, Sin. After everything we have done for her... Then she goes and does this stupid shit like we wouldn't find out. And she has been waiting on me hand and foot since that shit happened, with that guilty look on her face. She's broken my heart, but you can't kill her; that would kill my father."

"Kane, you can't act against her in anyway until I get home. I don't want Cuban to know we're on to him. I'll be home in about eight months. She's your enemy, so you have to keep her close to watch her. Well how is everything going with your security?"

"It's fine. The house feels like Fort Knox. But I do feel safe."

"Ma, I heard they hit you for five hundred g's."

"Yeah four hundred and ninety-five g's to be exact, Sin I promise I'll make it back."

"Nah, Kane, don't sweat it. I told Corletti the problem; he looking out."

"I know; his wife was in New York, so she came to see me with flowers and gifts. I just told everyone she was a client from the spa. She's a very nice person. Corletti sent his regards."

For the next forty-five minutes Sincere and Kisa discussed plans on how to get everything back on track. When the visitation was coming to a close, Kisa cried. Sincere fought back his urge to do the same. They kissed, hugged, and said goodbye.

Sincere went back to his cell without saying a word to anyone. As he lay on his bunk, he couldn't get the picture of Kisa's battered face out of his head. He knew Kisa meant what she said about not murdering Shea, but something had to be done. She had put his wife and unborn child in immediate danger. *Fuck whose daughter and sister she is*, he thought.

Sincere still had something to feel good about though. He smiled to himself as he thought about the surprise he had for Kisa.

Track 6: Back to the Way We Were

As autumn hung heavy over the city. Kisa felt good, even though she weighed nearly 200 pounds. It was the end of October and Kisa couldn't wait for November 4, her due date, Eisani, TaTa, Tyeis, and Shea had thrown huge baby shower at Justin's.

All of Kisa's closest family and friends were there. She had a wonderful time, and was truly overwhelmed by all the gifts she received. It took two trucks to get everything home. Kisa felt numb every time she had to look at Shea prancing around.

She hadn't even disclosed to Eisani that Shea was behind the robbery, because if Eisani knew, she would paralyze Shea. Eisani hated for anyone to fuck with Kisa. One night in the club a girl disrespected Kisa by throwing a drink in her face. Eisani beat her with a Cristal bottle, and cut her face with a broken Corona bottle. And that was just for throwing a drink in Kisa's face.

The more time Kisa had to spend around Shea the more disgusted she became. She couldn't wait for the issue to be resolved; she promised herself that she wouldn't let Sincere kill her. At least not while her father and Shea's mother were alive.

Even though she and Shea had different mothers, she loved and respected Shea's mother. And now that Kisa herself was with child, she could not appreciate the idea of taking a mother's daughter away from her.

Kisa put the finishing touches on the baby's nursery before moving back to Harlem to be closer to her doctor and the hospital. Eisani was now in charge of the money pick-ups, along with Terry providing security for her anytime she had more than $100,000.

Kisa gave Shea busy jobs to keep her away; she literally made Kisa sick to her stomach.

Kisa often stayed up nights watching her favorite movie *The Godfather II*. As she watched, her thoughts would drift back to falling in love with Sincere to the present. She would ask herself, *Is this my destiny? To run one of the most profitable cocaine rings this city has ever seen? And all by the age of twenty-one? What kind of future am I looking at?*

Kisa snapped out the self-twenty-question game that she was playing. She tried to enjoy the rest of the movie. She had a craving for Haagan Daz coffee ice cream.

She paused the DVD and got up to go into the kitchen. As she stood up, she felt a trickle down her leg, she thought it was urine. She cleaned herself and proceeded to the kitchen to fix herself a bowl of ice cream.

She sat back down and continued to watch the movie.

Then a pain hit her so hard, she dropped the brown ice cream on her cream carpet. That was followed by a big gush of liquid from her vagina.

"Fuck me! Terry, Terry I think I'm in labor," she screamed.

Terry ran into the room. The sight of Kisa leaking made him damn near pass out. A 6'6 270-pound tough guy could not bear seeing a woman in labor. "Kane, what do you need me to do?"

"I need you to get me a sweat suit from the closet, call E, and tell her to meet me at Harlem Hospital. My hospital bag is in her car."

Terry had done everything that Kisa had asked.

"Kane, what car do you want to take?"

"The five. I can't climb into the Range."

Kisa got to the hospital just in time. She had already fully dilated. One hour later, Madison Kai Montega was born, weighing 8-lbs. 11oz. She was twenty inches long. When Kisa saw her daughter's beautiful face, she forgot about all the labor pain.

She had Sincere's nose and Kisa's eyes and lips. Her hair was brown and like satin; it looked just like Kisa's hair on her baby pictures.

The next day Kisa's room was filled with family, friends, gifts and balloons. Everyone argued about who the baby looked like more, Kisa or Sincere.

Sincere's mother, Lena, and Kisa's mother, Demetria, would barely let anyone hold the baby-including Kisa. They only gave Kai to Kisa when it was time for her to be fed. She probably would not have gotten her then if she didn't breast feed.

Kisa grew weary of the hospital and begged the doctor to release her that evening. The first night out of the hospital, Kisa cried all night. She never had imagined this night with out Sincere.

Demetria and Lena helped her get through everything without extra stress. Things had been tense between Demetria and Kisa for the last couple of years. Demetria didn't agree with the way her oldest daughter had chosen to live.

Kisa was glad to have her mother there for the week; she hoped they would be able to mend their relationship a little. The baby helped smooth things over, but as always, they tried to avoid the inevitable conversation about Kisa's street life.

Now if people thought that Kisa and Eisani looked alike, they would swear that Demetria and Kisa were the same person. Kisa looked like her mother spit her out of her mouth. The only difference was Demetria was darker, her nose was narrower, and she was weighed ten pounds more than Kisa before the pregnancy.

Kisa loved her mother with all of her heart and soul. They were just alike but yet so very different. Both of them were so giving and very loyal. If you did right by them you had a friend for life. A strict, working family raised Demetria in a middle class neighborhood. Her parents instilled strong family values and good morals in her. In turn she instilled the same in Kisa; they were simply raised in a different era and environment.

The neighborhood Kisa was brought up in was rough and brutal. So instead of getting rolled over by the streets, she rolled with them. Demetria knew there was no use in complaining anymore; she knew it was in her daughter's blood.

On Kisa's father's side of the family, all of the boys hustled. Kisa had ways just like them. So it wasn't a big shock to Kisa's father, Mitch, or Demetria for that matter when she was expelled from high school for selling weed. From that day forward, it was clear to them why Kisa always kept money. Demetria could only hope and pray, now that Kai was here, that Kisa and Sincere would give up the street life. Kisa stood in the door and watched as her mother packed for her trip home.

"Mommy, I'm so glad you came. I'm going to miss you. Can you stay longer?"

"Baby, I wish I could spend more time with you and that beautiful baby. You know I have to get home to your father, the house, and your sister and brother. Besides, I was thinking you and Kai could come and spend a couple of weeks and Christmas with us, seeing that Sincere won't be here."

"Well we can come down the week of Christmas, but not a couple of weeks. I have too much to do around here."

"Like run your husband's drug ring? And nearly get yourself and your unborn child killed? I tried not to ruin this precious week for you in anyway, but this was bound to come up. Don't look so shocked; yeah I know everything that's going on around here. Did you think, because you're in the north and I'm in the south, I wouldn't know? It might be okay to tell Eisani everything, but you know TaTa tells their mother everything. And that's the worst part, I don't even hear it from you. I have to hear it from my loudmouth sister. Now I thought you and Sincere left all this behind."

Kisa walked over and sat on the bed next to the Louis Vuitton luggage she'd bought her mother the previous Christmas. She looked at it for a moment then at her mother. She began to speak as she fought hard to keep from crying.

"Mommy, I can't keep living a lie in your eyes. Yes I'm still living my life in a way that I'm not proud of. But soon all that will be over. I-"

"Kisa, baby, if you keep living this life you're living, there will be no *soon* for you." Her statement made the tears roll down Kisa's cheeks.

"Well, Mommy, pray for me? That's all I ask. Pray that I survive. Cause all this shit I go through right now, I go through it for everybody, I want everybody to live comfortable. Everybody got something to say about the way we made our money, but don't nobody mind taking it. Would you rather me be like you and struggle for fifteen to twenty years, wishing I lived in a better neighborhood. Please! That shit is like being in jail. The best thing those schools taught me, was that there are two kinds of people in this world: the fit and the unfit. And only the fittest survive. And, Mommy, you raised one of the fittest, most thoroughest women out here." Kisa stopped talking when she looked up and saw the tears coming from her mother's eyes. "Ma, I'm so sorry."

"No, Kisa, don't. You do not have to apologize for the way you feel. You have always been smart since you were a little girl, even wise beyond your years. So you already know there are consequences in this life. Look at me baby." She grabbed Kisa by the chin, like she was a little child.

"Look, in my eyes you are still that little baby that I brought home on that cold winter day. I held you close to my chest, wrapped tight in blankets, to protect you from that wind that was cutting like a knife. And ever since, I have spent countless nights and days worrying about you. I never know if I'm going to get a call from the police notifying me that my first born, the love of my life, is gone. And I have been living with that fear ever since you chose this life. That's a mother's pain and fear. The fear, that she will outlive her child. Now that you have that little girl in there, she needs you to be concerned for her well-being. She can't protect herself. You're in a war right now, and if you don't straighten up she will be a casualty of the war, which you and Sincere chose. Baby, all I am saying is for the sake of that child, get out while you can."

Eisani had been standing in the door too polite to interrupt. When Demetria stopped talking, she saw her chance. "Aunt D we have to go now, so you won't miss your flight. Terry already put your bags in the car, so come down when you get through."

Demetria wiped her eyes before turning to face her niece. "Yeah, baby, I'm ready. Come on, Kisa. Walk your old mother downstairs."

Kisa dried her face and followed her mother down stairs. Kisa helped her get into her coat.

Demetria turned and hugged her hard. "Baby, I don't hate you, and I'm not mad at you. Just please take heed to what I said. I love you so much. Take good care of my grandbaby."

Kisa had tears flowing down her face like a baby. She squeezed her mother hard. "I love you too Mommy."

"Bye, baby."

"Bye, Mommy." As Kisa let go she slipped three thousand dollars into her mommy's pocket.

Kisa closed the door and watched her mother into the car. She stood there Eisani's CLK disappeared. She ran upstairs, jumped in her bed, and had a good, long cry.

Days after Demetria had left, Kisa still felt like a lonely little girl, even though she had Lena and Eisani with her almost twenty-four hours a day. She missed Sincere badly; She talked to him everyday at least three times a day. She just could not talk to him like she really wanted to.

She tried not to sound sad; she didn't want to depress him with her problems. She loved telling him stories about Kai; she could tell in his voice that it made his day. Sincere could sense that she was trying to hide something. She wanted desperately to take Kai to see Sincere, but until she was a month old, she would have to settle for sending pictures.

The next two weeks breezed by. It was already Thanksgiving Thursday. Kisa's parents could not make it back, since Demetria had just visited for a week not long ago. This year, dinner was at Kisa's house. Sincere's mother, Lena, was still staying with Kisa to help out with the baby.

Lena was a very elegant lady. She and Kisa were very similar in appearance and mannerisms. Lena was still gorgeous. She looked thirty but was actually forty-nine. She and Kisa had become very close over the last year; they acted like two old friends. Lena would tell Kisa how she used to date all the old school hustlers back in her prime. She would tell Kisa, "That's when Harlem was really poppin', before crack fucked it up."

Lena loved Kisa like she was her own. She knew Kisa was good for her son and good to him. Lena's sisters came over early to help with dinner.

It was like a family reunion to them. They drank, gossiped, and laughed all day while preparing dinner. Everyone doted all over little Kai; she was already spoiled. Kisa fed Kai and laid her down for her four o'clock nap.

Kisa went into the bathroom to run her bath. When she walked back out into her bedroom, she stood by the window and watched the golden leaves falling to the ground. She smiled at the beauty of the scene. Her smiled faded quickly and turned into tears. She tried hard not to go into the postpartum depression everyone warned her about. But how could she not? She had not seen her husband in almost two months; they had a beautiful baby girl that he had not seen in person yet.

Kisa was more saddened by the fact that it was Thanksgiving Day, and Sincere had not called her. Lena watched Kisa from the bedroom door.

"Kane, baby, are you okay?"

"Yeah, Mommy, its just the holidays and Sin not being here. He has never even held Kai."

"Oh baby its okay to cry a little... Even a lot. Sometimes you have to let it out, if you hold it in, it can kill you. I loved Sincere's father so much. And when he was killed, I was three months pregnant with Sin. I only had five thousand dollars in the bank, and even in 1975 I could spend that on one outfit. I was so determined to do it all by myself, and I was very stubborn and adamant. I pushed myself and I never cried once until I got to my seventh month. I was so stressed out and angry ,I would wake up some days, wishing I were dead. That's the worst feeling in the world. One day I broke down, I cried for about five hours straight. After that I was a new person. So baby, don't be so hard that you can't cry. You know whenever you need to talk you can come to me. Now give me a hug; it's going to be okay. Everything will work out. Go take your bath and lie down for a while. If Kai wakes up I'll get her."

"Thank you, Mommy. I feel better already. I'm so glad you are here, I love you."

"I love you too. baby."

Kisa slid into the steaming hot bath water and sang along with Mary J.

"I can't help it if I wanted to /can't let you get away from me."

Listening to Faith and Mary always got Kisa's mind right. To her, they kept it so real. Both of them were from the hood, and their pain was real, not manufactured. The music soothed her so much she fell asleep in the tub. When she woke up the water was cold, her skin was all wrinkled, and it was a quarter to six.

"Ah shit!" She yelled as she bumped her knee getting out of the tub.

Kisa had not lost all her weight; she had about five pounds to go. Yet she still didn't feel comfortable wearing anything to close to her body. So she decided on a pair of rich blue Dolce and Gabbana jeans, and a burnt orange and beige Dolce and Gabbana hooded sweater. She was comfortable with wearing heels again so she wore a pair of brown 'gator boots with a flat high-heel. She pulled her hair in a straight back ponytail. She decided on no make up, just a little gloss and lip liner.

Kisa felt better with these clothes on. It was a far cry from all the maternity clothes, big sweat suits, and oversized T-shirts she had worn for the last ten months. Looking in the mirror at her own appearance even cheered her up.

"I'm almost back," she told herself smiling. When Kisa walked out of her bedroom she could hear a lot more talking than earlier. She knew that the guest had arrived. She walked over to Kai's nursery. She opened the door, didn't see Kai in her crib, and panicked. Then she remembered Lena had her.

She walked down the stairs slowly; when she got to the bottom she was relieved to see Nana, Sincere's grandmother, holding Kai.

"Hi, Nana."

"Hi, baby. How are you feeling today?"

"I'm doing fine, Nana, and you?"

"Oh, baby, you know this old lady is just trying to make it."

"Oh please, Nana, you know you still got it."

Lena stepped out of the kitchen looking glamorous in a beige pantsuit that draped nicely over her petit frame. "Well I see Kane has joined us. We can sit down for dinner. Kisa, tell Terry and Slim to come in and have some dinner. They don't have to guard that damn yard on Thanksgiving Day."

Everyone gathered in the dining room. When Nana started the grace there was a loud, heavy knock on the door. Kisa started towards the living room. Terry told her to stay put. Terry and Slim went into the living room. The dining room was completely silent until Terry called for Kisa to come into the living room.

Kisa prayed to herself. "Please don't let this be the police starting with me on Thanksgiving." When she got in the living room she could not believe her eyes.

"Bay, what are you doing home? How did you get out? I don't care. Come here! Hug me, kiss me, and let me know I'm not dreaming."

"Baby, you are not dreaming, ma, I'm home," Sincere said as he embraced his wife.

Tears streamed from Kisa's eyes as they engaged in a long deep kiss. Kisa heard everyone come into the living room behind her, but she didn't want to let her man go. She slowly pulled away when she heard Lena behind her.

"Can I get a little hug from my son?"

"You sure can, I just had to make sure it was real."

Kisa pulled away slowly and walked over to Butta. "What's up, my nigga? Give me a hug. Y'all niggas could have called to tell me you were coming home."

Butta displayed his Mr. America smile, glad to see his play-sister looking good, despite what she had went through during her pregnancy. "Ma, you know that nigga; he wanted to surprise you. He wouldn't let us tell anybody we were coming home. But I am so happy to see you healed up beautifully."

"Thanks, Butta."

"Kane, where my daughter at?" Sincere yelled from across the room.

"Nana has her in the Dining room."

Sincere walked into the dining room and hugged his Nana. When he took Kai into his arms, he simply stared into her eyes. She was the most beautiful thing he had ever seen.

He turned to Kisa. "Can we go upstairs for a minute?"

"Sure, baby. Everyone please excuse us. Go ahead and start eating. Don't wait for us."

On the way out, Sincere hugged his family. He missed them all terribly, but he needed to be alone with his wife and new child.

Kisa led Sincere into Kai's nursery.

"Ma, this is nice. You did this all by yourself?"

"I sure did."

"Kane, Kai is so beautiful. She looks just like you."

"Nah, poppi, I think she has those funny-colored brown eyes like you."

Sincere paced around the room holding Kai. Kisa sat in a rocking chair next to the crib.

"Sincere, please tell me you didn't bust out?"

"Girl, you don't believe that shit!"

"Well how did you get out this soon? And why didn't you tell me?"

"Ma, you know that nigga Mazetti got connects everywhere. Him and the big man from corrections are dumb tight. After we got sentenced he hit that nigga wit some cake and told us to stick it out for at least seven to nine months so it wouldn't look shady. I didn't tell you 'cause Mommy told me you were walking around all depressed and shit. So I thought if I surprised you it would cheer you up. Ah, shit, Kisa what's wrong? She is throwing up!"

"She's fine. She just ate and you're walking around bouncing her. Hand her here; let me clean her up and change her."

Sincere watched Kisa and felt like Kai brought out a gentleness in her that he had never noticed about her before.   He thought to himself, *That bitch Shea and Joe almost kept me from seeing this.* He snapped out his trance. "So, Kane, where is Shea?"

"I don't know, probably on her way. Why?"

"I just wanted to know."

"Sin, I know you want to take care of this soon, but you just came home to us."

"Ma, nothing is going to happen right now. We're in the process of going through everything, planning shit carefully so it goes smooth. I'm going to lay low in the house for about a month, with you and Kai. Lets talk about all that tomorrow. Anyway, baby, how are you feeling? I told you I didn't want you to be moping."

Kisa put Kai in her crib and walked over to Sincere and sat on his lap.

"Poppi, I'm great now that you are here. I feel like a million ton of bricks have been lifted off my shoulders. I feel free now that you're here. I can rest again."

"Bay I hope you don't mind but I need you and Eisani to keep running everything for a while 'cause you know the jakes is going to be watching me."

"Only a minute, Sin. I mean I'm tired of doing this shit, and I want you to stop too. Listen, I know how much we're really bringing in, and its way more than I thought, which is more than enough for us to live off of for the rest of our lives."

"Look, ma, just a few more years. I have no choice. Forget all that for now you know what I need." Sincere began to unzip Kisa's jeans.

She politely pushed his hand away and zipped her jeans. "Whoa now. Slow down I just had a baby three and a half weeks ago. I still have to wait another two and a half weeks before I can even think about having sex."

"Come on Ma just a little bit."

"Boy, no! I have to wait for my hormones to drop, I'm too fertile right now, and I'm not trying to get pregnant again."

"What you trying to say? You wouldn't give me another seed?"

"Not really and especially not right now!"

"What does that mean?"

"Look, Sincere, pregnancy was no joke. It was hard and exhausting and I don't know if I could go through it again. Now if you act like a good boy, I'll give you some nice slow head. After everyone leaves and after I give you a long hot bath to wash that Rikers smell off of you."

"Aight, ma, I'll accept that."

"I know you will."

"Don't be a smart-ass, Miss."

"Sin, please just hold me for a while, so I can feel that it's real."

They sat and cuddled for an hour just watching their daughter sleep.

When Kai woke up, Sincere and Kisa returned to the dining room.

"Well I didn't think you all were going to join us," remarked Lena, smiling ear-to-ear, so glad to have her boys home.

At that moment Shea entered the dining room.

Kisa's heart dropped. She looked directly at Sincere to see his reaction; he was already on top of his game.

"What's up, Shea? How you been?" He asked with a smirk on his face.

Kisa knew that smirk. To anyone else it looked like a slight smile, but Kisa knew it meant trouble.

"Sincere, I'm chillin' as always. I know you're glad to be home sweetie."

"You know I am, shorty, always ready to get back down to business."

"Okay, okay," Lena interrupted, "My boy needs to eat now."

Dinner was the most fun Kisa had had in a long time. Everyone laughed, joked and told stories well past midnight. Having Sincere, Butta, Mannie and Shawn home made it even better.

After cleaning the kitchen, upon Lena's demand, the house cleared out around two o'clock. Lena took control of Kai for the night so Kisa and Sincere could have some time alone.

Sincere walked into the room and busted out laughing at the sight of Kisa pumping milk out of her breast. "Kisa, what in the hell is that?"

"Shut up, stupid! I'm pumping milk so Mommy will have some bottles for Kai tonight."

"That shit looks too funny."

"Sin, you better leave me the fuck alone before I change my mind. Now go on upstairs; I'll be up as soon as I finish."

Kisa finished up and joined Sincere in the bathtub. Kisa bathed him good from head to toe, dried him, and rubbed him down with lotion.

Then Kisa took all of him into her mouth, making love to his manhood with her tongue. Sincere could not hold back; it had been so long since he had had an orgasm. As he came, Kisa did something she had never done before- she swallowed it all.

Sincere felt completely drained after that long awaited orgasm, he really wanted to get inside of Kisa. Kisa washed her face, brushed her teeth and slipped into a sheer nightgown, something she had not bothered to wear in the last ten months. She felt warm and secure lying in Sincere's arms. Sincere felt relieved by her sense of relief.

"Kane, our daughter is so beautiful. Ma, I'll never leave you two again. I can't even believe we made her."

"She is my little angel," Kane replied. "I can't even stand being away from her. When they handed her to me in the hospital I could not stop crying. They wanted her to go to the nursery, but I wasn't for it. I have never been away from her more than four hours. Now that I have her, I could never imagine life without her."

"Baby I can't even imagine life without you. And now that I'm home, we can go back to the way we were."

Kisa easily fell asleep in the comfort of Sincere's arm. He didn't go so easily. He kept seeing Shea's fake-ass coming through that door. It made his blood boil, although he'd kept his composure. He really wanted to snap her little shiesty neck. He didn't worry. He had something planned for her ass and Butta was setting it all in motion.

Back in the city, Butta and Shea were getting reacquainted. She could never resist his advances. He looked like he was a mere pretty-ass Dominican nigga with cornrows. He was far from that. He was as rough and rugged as they came.

Lena had basically raised him since he was ten. His father was doing life upstate for a murder, and his mother was only worried about her next hit of heroin. Lena started out feeding him everyday because she could tell he wasn't being fed.

One morning, around four o'clock, Lena was on her way home from the Lenox Lounge when she saw

Butta outside on a school night. She scooped him up and raised him as her own.

Butta took Sincere's problems as his own. He felt when Sincere had beef, so did he. He also loved Kisa like a real sister. He would do anything for her, and vice versa. Even before Kisa and Sincere hooked up Butta and Kisa had a good friendship.

Even though both of them were very attractive, they never looked at each other in a sexual way. Lena, Sincere, Kisa, and Kai were the only family he knew and anyone who jeopardized that would feel some serious repercussions.

He abhorred Shea for setting Kisa up to be robbed, but he had to stick to the script so Sincere's plan would work. On top of that, he didn't mind getting some ass in the process. Butta was just happy that the family was back together again.

Track 7: Another Birthday!

Sincere had quietly planned Kisa a big birthday bash. He would have asked her, but he didn't want her saying no again. Plus Sincere needed to use her party as an official homecoming party. Sincere and his crew had not been out since their release from prison. The entire month of December they all laid low at Sincere and Kisa's house.

Christmas and New Years were very private for them. There was almost no limit to what Kai received for Christmas. She was barely a month old, and had over fifty gifts under the tree. Kisa had only bought her five of the gifts. She felt Kai was too young to understand. But it was useless trying to explain that to Sincere. He felt like Kai deserved the world.

When Sincere and Butta came through the door on Christmas Eve with all those gifts, Kisa protested, "Sincere, Kai does not need all of this. She will not even know what's going on. She won't even remember this Christmas."

"That is why I'm going to tape it."

Kisa walked off mumbling, "I give up. I'm going to bed."

"Are we still exchanging gifts at midnight?"

"Yeah, just wake me up."

When the clock struck twelve, Sincere hollered upstairs for Kisa to come down. "Yo, Kane, it's twelve o'clock. Come on."

She came down complaining, "Are you crazy boy? Don't be up in here hollering and shit. You know if you wake Kai up you not going to be the one up with her."

"Hush girl and come over here."

Kisa went and stood next to the tree with Sincere. He pulled her close and just held her without saying anything.

"Sin, baby, are you okay?"

"Yeah, ma, I'm fine. I'm just happy to be home for Christmas. This one is so special. That's why I bought Kai so much, just in case I don't get to see another one."

Kisa stood on her tiptoes and kissed him. "Baby, we are going to have so many more Christmases together." She bent down and retrieved a black and silver gift bag from underneath the tree, and handed it to Sincere.

He bent down to get hers and she stopped him.

"No, Sin, open yours first."

He opened the box and simply smiled. "Ma, this so special. I love it." She had given him a Byzantine-cut platinum chain and a charm with Kai's birth date in diamond baguettes. He truly loved his gift, but he was so excited about what he had bought her, that he could not wait any longer to give it to her. He handed her a funny-shaped box with two compartments. He was smiling so hard he was almost laughing. "Go ahead open this side first."

She opened the larger side of the shiny black tin box. When she opened it she didn't exactly frown, but her facial expression was one of bewilderment. Inside was a mini-size replica of a pearl white Mercedes Benz S-Class 600. Kisa didn't know what to say without hurting Sincere's feelings. "I like it, Sin. What is it though a collector's item?"

"Something like that."

Kisa took it out the box and eyed it some more. He could tell by the expression on her face, that she wasn't feeling the gift.

"Ma you have to open the other side to get a real feel for it."

Kisa opened the smaller side of the box inside she found a solid white gold Mercedes emblem key chain, and two Mercedes keys. She looked up at Sin.

"Okay, Sin, what am I suppose to do with this."

"Turn the key chain over and read it."

She flipped the key chain over. It was engraved around the circle. She read the engraving.

Wifey's 6, Love, Sincere Xmas 2000.

She looked at the mini 600 and then at Sincere.

"Okay, what is this?"

Sincere was still smiling ear-to-ear

"Look at the tag on the car."

Kisa took the car out of the box and read the tag; it read *Wifey's 6.*

"See, that's your personalized plates."

"So this is my Christmas gift? A replica 600 and a key chain."

He grabbed her by the hand and pulled her to the window.

He pulled the curtains back. "No, that's just a replica of your Christmas gift," he said, pointing out the window.

She looked out the window and began jumping up and down, screaming. Outside, in the yard, Butta and Mannie were standing next to a new Mercedes S-Class 600. It was Pearl white just like the toy car. It had the same tag, eighteen-inch chrome rims, and it was wrapped in a big red bow. Kisa was truly surprised. "Sin, you bought this for us?"

"No, ma, I copped it for you."

Kisa jumped up and hugged Sincere's neck. "Thank you, baby, I love it. Sin, you make my gift look so little."

"Baby, you've given me the best gift over the last three years. Nothing materialistic could measure up to what you have given me. I know this past year has been so stressful for you, I just wanted to give you something to show you how much I appreciate everything."

"Ah, Sin, you know that I know you're appreciative. Bay, this is so sweet. I'm going to slip my clothes back on. I want to drive it."

Kisa ran upstairs and put on the jean suit with the mink trim that she had been wearing earlier that day.

Kisa made her way outside to get a closer look at her new car. Sincere opened the car door for her. The inside was so beautiful she wanted to cry. It had a smoked gray interior, wood grain dash and gear column, and Kisa's initials were stitched in the headrest.

Sincere showed her how to use the navigation system, the DVD, and the phone. Kisa wasn't interested in all of that at the moment; she just wanted to take it for a spin.

"Aight, Sin, you can show me all that tomorrow. Let me see how it rides."

Kisa pulled away from the curb slowly, and then gave it some gas. It rode so smooth but yet so powerful. She was doing forty in a twenty-five and it felt like she wasn't moving. She sped around the neighborhood a few times then she decided she wanted to drive it to the city.

She dialed Eisani's number from her new mobile phone. Eisani didn't pick up after five rings; Kisa forgot that she wouldn't answer if she didn't recognize the number. So she kept calling and letting the phone ring until Eisani answered with an attitude.

"Who is this?"

"Eisani, its Kane."

"Oh, what up, ma? What number are you calling from?"

"This is the number to the phone in my car."

"You got a phone put in the Range?"

"Something like that. Look, I'm on my way to the city I have something to show you."

"Is it important? We're on our way out."

"Yes, it is important, and who is *we?*"

"TaTa, Tyeis, and me."

"Well stay there; I'm on my way."

"No, you have to meet us at the Copa Cabana, 'cause we're already late."

"What's so important at the Copa tonight, on Christmas Eve?"

"It's Big June's party, and SnS' birthday."

Kisa's other line beeped. She desperately tried to figure how to click over.

"Look, this is Sin on the other line, and I don't even know how to click over on this phone. So I'll meet you in front of the club in ten minutes. One."

After nearly crashing into the tollbooth, she figured out how to answer the call.

"Hello?"

"Kane, where the hell you at? You've been gone for twenty minutes."

"I'm on my way to the city to meet E. I'll be home soon."

"Kane, don't go to the city."

"Too late, I just paid the toll. I'm already on the bridge."

"You can still turn around."

"Bye, Sin!"

Kisa pressed the end button and turned on the stereo. She tuned it to Hot 97, and turned it all the way up. She danced and sang along with the mix.

Damn Cipher Sounds is doing his thing. He was playing all her favorites from the summer like Mystikal's *Shake Ya Ass,* Shyne's *Bad Boys,* and Cam' Ron's *What Means The World to You.*

Kisa pulled up to the block where the club was located, and it was packed. She slowly inched up to the front of the club. Everyone looked on, wondering who was driving that 600.

She spotted Eisani, TaTa and Tyeis standing on the curb. She pulled right up on them, they all looked at the car trying to see who was inside. Kisa slowly let the window down. They all smiled when they saw it was Kisa. Eisani walked over to the window.

"Bitch, whose car you done went and stole."

"Bitch, read the tags. Okay its mine, and my husband gave it to me for Christmas."

"Ma, this is beautiful," Tyeis said.

"Thank you, baby."

TaTa was genuinely happy for her little cousin. "Kane, this is nice. Baby you really deserve it."

Kisa knew TaTa was talking about everything from the past year. She didn't want to get too emotional so she kept it short. "Thanks, Ta, well I'm not going to hold y'all up any longer. I better get home to my husband before he kills me."

Eisani wanted Kisa to come and party with them like old times. "Ma, come inside with us for a little while. And don't say you have to get home to Kai, cause I know Lena is there with her."

"Girl, I'm not dressed. And I am going home to be with my husband. And I'm going to give him as much as he wants tonight. So see you girls tomorrow."

January came in quietly, as did the New Year for Kisa and Sincere. Kisa's birthday fell on a Wednesday.

Sincere gave her more decorations for her wrist. He gave her a Presidential Rolex to replace her Carrier, and a diamond charm bracelet from Kai.

Kisa was in love with the bracelet. It already had two charms on it, a diamond baby bottle, and a diamond half-heart. Sincere gave her five thousand dollars to get something to wear for dinner.

"But make sure it's something you can wear to the club; we're meeting everyone at club Aria after dinner," he told her.

Kisa, Lena, and Kai hopped into Kisa's new 600 and headed to the city. They looked city-glamorous in their jeans, minks, and shoe boots as they shopped on Fifth Ave.

Kisa chose a red leather Capri suit by Diane Von Fastener. She felt comfortable with her choice since she had lost all her extra weight. She couldn't find any boots in midtown, so they headed for the Village to her favorite store, Petit Peton. Kisa instantly picked out a pair of stiletto boots with different color red patches all over. When Kisa left the store she saw Shea with some girls. They were going into Limpase'.

"Yo, Shea, what's poppin?"

"Oh, what up, Kane? What you down here coppin?"

"I just came to get some boots to wear tonight."

"Oh yeah, Butta told me we're supposed to meet y'all tonight at the club."

"Yeah. Well let me get out of here; Lena and Kai are in the car waiting."

Kisa looked in the direction of the car, so Shea and her friends looked in the same direction. Shea had been out of town for the holidays, so she didn't know Sincere had bought Kisa the car.

Kisa could see the jealousy all in Shea's face. After Shea closed her mouth. "When did you get that, bitch?"

"Sin gave it to me for Christmas."

"So I know you didn't get nothing for your birthday!"

"Yes, I did! Sin and Kai gave me this," Kisa said, showing off her wrist.

"But, girl, let me go so Ty can give me a fresh doobie. And, oh yeah! Chic, you didn't even tell your lil' sister happy birthday."

"My bad. Happy b-day, Kane. I was looking for your gift right now. I mean it ain't gon' be no rolley or six, but I got you, ma."

Kisa walked on to the car.

Shea told her girls, "That's one spoiled bitch."

Kisa headed uptown to the salon, dropping Lena and Kai off at Nana's house. When she walked into the Salon, balloons and birthday cake greeted her. Her favorite cousins came out of the office singing *Happy Birthday* with gifts in hand.

Kisa hugged them all and said, "I love you bitches! Thank you so much."

"Come on," Tyeis said, leading her towards the shampoo bowl. "Let me wash your hair right quick so you can open your presents while I roll your hair."

Eisani and TaTa sat in chairs close to Tyeis's booth while she rolled Kisa's hair. Eisani told Kisa, "Open my gift first ma."

Kisa gasped when she saw the red Gucci bag.

"We must really be twins, E. I just bought a red leather suit for tonight. Thank you, ma-ma, I love it."

"Anything for you twin."

Eisani winked at Kisa.

Kisa reached for the next gift bag.

"Now I can't wait to see what Miss TaTa got me, and this bag is big, so I know it's good. And it's two boxes in here. What could this be?"

Kisa could not believe it when she saw the lime green Christian Dior ostrich jacket and bag. "Chick, I went looking for this today and they said they were sold out. Thank you baby. Now I have to go cop the boots too."

"No you don't," Tyeise said handing her another box.

"I know you didn't, little girl!"

"Yes I did!"

Sure enough when Kisa opened the box, she saw the matching boots.

"You bitches are the best! Y'all did not have to do all this."

"Yeah we did!" Tyeise remarked, kissing her cousin on the cheek.

"I have too many gifts. More shit than I need."

"Oh boy," Eisani sighed. "What did Sin give you?"

"Oh you didn't see my new wrist wrappery, nigga?" Kisa asked pulling back her sleeve.

"That is a beautiful bracelet." TaTa remarked.

Tyeise looked closer and her eyes widened.

"He gave you the Presidential Rolley! Get it, bitch!"

"Oh yeah!" Kisa said while sitting up real attentive. "You know I saw Shea and some next bitches in the Village today."

Eisani spun around in her seat. "And what did that bitch have to say?"

"Well you know I had not talked to her since Thanksgiving. She went to Miami for the holidays with some nigga. Needless to say, she didn't know I had the new six. Y'all should have seen her face. Then she told

me, I know that's your Christmas and Birthday too. So
you know I had to flash my wrist on her! You should
have seen the way her and those bitches gagged. And
to top that off, that bitch knew it was my birthday and
didn't say shit to me. I had to tell her, 'oh you not gon'
tell me happy birthday?'"

"And what did she say?" Asked TaTa.

"Oh you know she copped out wit her fake ass
and was wit the 'happy birthday, lil' sis.' Talking
about I'm going to get your gift now."

"She is so fuckin grimy and phony," Eisani
hissed.

"And I bet not find out she had anything to do
with setting us up. If I do I'm gon' choke her ass out."

"Calm down, E. You know she gon be at the
club tonight. Anyway, on to better things. What yall
wearing tonight?"

"Girl, I don't even know. I'm going to get
something after I get a piece of cake." TaTa answered.

"I'm going with you, 'cause I don't have
anything," Eisani said.

"Aight, E and Ta, I'll check y'all tonight."

"Aight Kisa. Where you going when you leave
here?" asked TaTa, with a mouth full of cake.

"I have to pick Lena and Kai up from Nana's
house and get back to Jersey. Sin is taking me out to
eat before we go to the club."

Kisa had dozed off from the warm heat of the
dryer. The clicking sound of the dryer woke Kisa up.

"Ty, my hair is dry."

"Are you sure, Kane?"

"Girl, I know and I was under for an hour without getting up!"

"Well come on and let me take your rollers out."

"Ty just wrap me and pin me up; I have to get out of here. And what time are you leaving today?"

"In about an hour after I brush my last client down and clean up."

"Well I know you coming to the club tonight."

"Ma, I wouldn't miss it for shit."

Tyeis finished with Kisa's hair; Kisa gathered her things so she could leave.

"Thank you for everything, Ty."

"You welcome, girl. I'll get the cake and walk you out to the car."

Tyeis and Kisa were putting everything in the trunk when a silver Excursion pulled next to them. Kisa could not see who was inside because of the silver mirror tints on the windows. This made her tense, so she gripped the glock .380 she had hidden in her coat pocket.

When the window rolled down her heart sank, not out of fear but because it was the only other man she had ever loved. And the only man to ever break her heart. It had been more than two and a half years since she had last saw him in person. He now ran his own thriving record company, Bricklayers Entertainment. He also had his hand in many other ventures that kept him in the media spotlight. She often saw him on BET, MTV, or in Magazines.

It took her a long time to get past the heartache he'd caused her. Kisa was with him and stood by him the entire time when he had nothing. When he was struggling to get his business going, Kisa supported him financially and emotionally. The more he came up and got his business together, the more he disrespected their relationship.

It killed Kisa when she caught him in Cancun during Memorial Day weekend with some bum bitch. That was all she could take. She flew back to New York and moved in with Eisani. He begged for her to come home for three months. Kisa would not accept his phone calls. If she saw him out she would ignore him. Soon his attitude became *fuck her,* and he moved on.

He had been thinking about her a lot lately and seeing her now made him realize how much he still loved her and how much he really wanted her back.

Yeah, he could have anyone he wanted, and basically he had. But he knew that ninety-eight percent of them just wanted his paper. Like, Sincere, he too knew that Kisa loved him with or with out the paper. He knew she was married to Sincere and how dangerous that was, but he had to try his luck with a little flirting.

The moment was tense for the both of them. The only people who understood this were Tyeis and his brother who was in the driver seat. His artist and entourage, who were in the truck looked on awkwardly.

So Kisa broke the Silence. "Now, Coco, you know you can get shot rolling up on me like that."

"Nah, ma, I know you could never blast a nigga as pretty as me."

Kisa pulled the glock out of her pocket and held it in a downward position next to her thigh. "Why couldn't I?"

Flashing his golden-boy smile he responded.

"'Cause you could never live with yourself, knowing you hurt something this pretty!"

"I see you the same old Coco."

"Ma, ain't nothing changed, but my bank account," he said as he got out of the truck.

"Yeah, whatever, nigga."

"I see you still fly and gorgeous, shortly."

"I wouldn't have it no other way, *fam*

"Oh, so you that fly now, you call a nigga fam! And a nigga can't even get a hug. That's so fucked up."

It was this cockiness that had attracted Kisa to him, and his style. Coco had always been a fly-ass nigga and that is one thing Kisa loved.

"Yeah, I guess you can have a hug, but don't be coppin'" no feels." When she hugged him he smelled so good, he was wearing Aqua Di Gio. A fragrance she loved when she was with him and hated when she left him. Sincere used to wear it until she told him how she hated it. He stopped wearing it, not knowing it reminded her of Coco. Kisa only bought him Issey Miyaki and Eternity.

Tyeis interrupted the moment. "Kane, I'm out, so I can get finished. Happy birthday again. Give me a hug. Be safe, ma," Tyeis said with a hint of Sarcasm in her voice.

"I will, and thanks again lil' mama."

Tyeis turned around. "Club Aria right?"

As Tyeis was walking off a voice called out from the Excursion.

"Yo, shorty, where you going? Let me holla at you for a minute."

A young, good-looking boy called out to Tyeis. He got out the truck with an oversized Sean John snorkel on.

"Well you better come walk with me, 'cause I'm not coming back over there." Tyeis yelled back, sounding like the teenager she actually was. Kisa smiled as she watched him chase her little cousin up the block. She turned back to Coco. He was still smiling like he was in a daze.

"How have you been, Co?"

"I have been great and you?"

"Life has been good, and I'm not wanting for anything."

"I can see that. Nice fur, wrist and ears icy, and a new six."

"Nah, nigga, that's not what I'm talking about, I have a new daughter who brings me a lot of joy. I'm late picking her up."

"You have a seed that's not mine? You know you were suppose to have mine first."

"Well you fucked that up, didn't you?"

"Ma, I don't want to even get into those memories right now; It's a new day. Happy belated birthday baby," Coco said, handing her a card."

"A lil' something for you to buy yourself something nice."

Kisa looked down at the card. "So it wasn't a coincidence that you saw me here."

"I was carrying it around hoping I would run into you. You know I miss you, Kane."

"Look, Corick, you know I'm married to Sincere now, and I love him and even more, I respect him. So please don't go there, and here I can't accept this."

"No, Kane, you keep that, if only out of the friendship we used to have. It's just a gift."

The boy who had been talking to Tyeis ran back up the block. "Yo, we have to go to Aria tonight. Shorty is going to be there. Co, she is mean, I have to see her tonight duke."

"Aight, man, calm down. We may swing by after your photo shoot. That's if it's alright with the birthday girl."

"Coco, it's a free country and an open club." Kisa really didn't care if he came. She knew he wouldn't dare do anything stupid in the presence of Sincere.

"Well maybe we will bump into each other tonight."

"Maybe," Kisa remarked as she got into her car.

"I'll holla," Coco said as he got into his truck.

As they pulled off, his artist Young Gunna asked, "Yo, who was that? She is a dime, I know you hittin' that!"

"Nah, baby boy, it ain't even like that. That's my old wifey."

"Your old wiz? Nigga, you need to get back at that. Shit she pushin' that six and I know she got paper."

"Yeah, my baby always did her thing, but she's married now."

"Nigga you are Coco you're a millionaire, you better herb that nigga, and claim what's yours."

"My young nigga, it's not that simple. She's married to Sincere Montega."

That ended that conversation quickly.

Kisa sat in the car and watched Coco's truck pull off. She looked down at the card; she decided to read it before she picked up Lena and Kai. The card contained twenty-one, $100 bills.

The card read: *Sometimes in Life we let the really important people get away. Once there gone, we realize how unhappy life is without them. No matter what else we may have. This is an expression of how much I'm missing you. Love Always and Happy, Happy Birthday, Coco. P.S. If you ever need anything at all, call me. 917-555-8090*

Kisa put the cash in her purse, ripped the card, threw it out the window, and pulled off.

Kisa and Sincere had a nice quiet dinner at Jezebels. When Kisa got inside of Club Aria, she was truly surprised. She could not believe Sin was able to pull this off without someone leaking it to her. She really thought they were just going to meet the crew.

She was overwhelmed when everyone yelled, *"Surprise."*

Sincere liked surprising her and he had an even bigger surprise for her after the party. Everyone was there just the way he had planned it. He wanted to know who had come up and who was really doing it in the game.

Sincere and Kisa sat at two different VIP tables. Sincere, Butta, Mannie, Shawn and about five other guys sat at one table. Kisa, Eisani, Tyeis, and TaTa had their own table. Shea came through with her crew. She sat for a while then left. In all actuality, she left because she was disgusted by all the attention Kisa was receiving.

When Sincere saw Shea leaving, he told Butta, "Go make sure she knows she is to leave here with you tonight."

Both tables were filled with Cristal, Belvedere, Remy, and Moet, along with glasses of mixed drinks. Young rich music industry execs and rappers were hanging out at Sincere's table, laughing and having a good time.

Sincere looked up once and saw Kisa talking to Mary J. Blige, Latanya Blige-DeCosta and Eve. He sat thinking how well she fit in with them; she looked like she should be in their world. She looked like a hip-hop star instead of a major drug dealer. He just stared at her with a blank stare, that is, until something broke his gaze. He saw Coco walk over to Kisa's table and speak; he was with three other guys and a bodyguard.

The younger guy walked away from the table with Tyeis.

Coco spoke to everyone at Kisa's table and kept it moving. He walked towards Sincere's table; he spoke to everyone he knew, or really everyone who knew him. When he got to Sincere they gave each other dap. Only the people who knew them both, personally, could feel the tension. Kisa watched the exchange intensely while holding her breath.

When Coco walked away, Sincere and Kisa made eye contact. That made Kisa very uneasy. She turned her head quickly. Sincere wondered what had brought Coco around all of a sudden. But he knew his baby would never cheat, so he quickly erased those thoughts.

Half an hour later Sincere spotted Kisa laying the Cristal and blunts on pretty thick.

"Yo, ma, slow down," he told her.

"For what? It's my birthday, and I thought you liked me full of Cris'."

"Yeah, ma, I do, but I got another surprise for you tonight, and I don't need you to be pissy."

"Okay, baby. Oh, Sin, that's my song! Come on, let's dance."

"Nah, baby, you go ahead I'm gonna sit back down. But we're leaving in about forty-five minutes."

Kisa walked towards the dance floor, singing, *"I never knew a love like this before, never knew, never knew."*

Kisa danced and danced. It seemed like SnS was playing all of her songs. Then he threw on Jay-Z's *"I Just Want To Love You."*

Kisa really started getting it. Coco stood on the side of the dance floor watching the way Kisa moved. He stared at her, thinking of how she used to move when they made love.

Coco wanted to grab her and dance with her, but she was Sincere's wife and he was there. He wasn't afraid of Sincere, because by no means was Coco a punk. He just didn't want to cause any trouble for Kisa; he loved her and respected her too much for that.

It had been over an hour since Sincere had told Kisa to be ready to leave. He walked around looking for her, then he saw Eisani.

"Yo, Eisani, you seen Kisa?"

"You know she on the dance floor."

"Well come on and get her things; we'll get her on the way out."

"Why are we leaving already?"

"I have a surprise for y'all. Now come on Butta and them already there."

Sincere and Eisani Spotted Kisa in the middle of the dance floor grooving. Sincere also spotted Coco gazing at Kisa. Eisani was getting ready to go get her when Sincere pulled her back. "That's okay E. I'll go get her."

Sincere walked over to Kisa and hugged her up. "Baby, I know you're having fun, but we have to go now."

"Okay, baby, let me get my stuff."

"Eisani already has your things. Come on, she's waiting for us."

As they walked away, Sincere wrapped his arm around her waist and kissed her while looking towards Coco. Sincere gave him a look that said, *you can stop thinking about it nigga!*

Shawn was waiting outside for them in a rented Suburban. Sincere directed Kisa and Eisani towards the truck.

Kisa, in her tipsy demeanor, looked at Sincere funny and asked, "Sincere, where is my car?"

"Mannie took it to the house.   Stop asking fucking questions and get in the truck."

"Who the fuck you cursing at?   Shit, you get on my fuckin' nerves."

Kisa and Sincere rode in the back, while Eisani sat up front with Shawn. Sincere wasn't drunk, but he had had a few drinks, so he was feeling himself.

He leaned over to Kisa and whispered, "What the fuck was Coco doing there?"

Kisa looked at him and rolled her eyes. "Sin don't fuckin' start wit me, 'cause I isn't for it!"

Sincere grabbed her arm and pulled her close. "Who the fuck you talking to like that?" he asked her with a harsh tone.

Kisa was not feeling his mood. "Sincere, let me go; I'm not fucking playing. Now let me go. That's your own guilt you're feeling, cause ain't nobody fucking with Coco."

Sincere squeezed into her arm a little harder.   "I better not hear shit about you and Coco, or I'm gonna beat your ass with wire hangers."   He jerked her arm so violently, when he let her go she hit the door. Eisani and Shawn didn't even get involved; they knew it was best to leave them two alone when they fought seriously.

Kisa leaned against the door and fell asleep.

Sincere felt stupid for doing that, but he had to make himself clear about the situation. He thought to himself , *Why am I buggin'? I know my baby ain't going nowhere.*

He slid close to Kisa and put his arm around her.

She woke up and pushed him away.   "Stop Sincere, I don't feel like being bothered, as a matter of fact, you can take me home."

"Ma, stop acting like that."

"No, Sin, I really don't feel like being bothered, and you completely blew my high."

Sincere just left her alone. They rode another twenty minutes on Route 1 and 9 before Shawn pulled in to what appeared to be an abandoned business park.

Kisa and Eisani looked at each other. Then Kisa looked at Sincere. "What is this shit?"

He smiled devilishly. "A surprise, lil' mama, a big surprise."

When they pulled around to the back, Kisa saw Butta and Terry's trucks parked in the back. When they walked in Kisa shivered from the cold and damp air on the inside.

As they walked towards the back of the building, she could see a man tied up by his hands, which were suspended in the air, and he was barely standing on his feet. As she got closer she realized it was Cuban Joe.

Sincere walked up behind her. "Baby, I told you I had a big surprise." Then he yelled out, "Yo Mannie bring that bitch out here!"

Kisa turned around as they brought Shea from another room, blindfolded with her hands tied behind her back. She had been roughed up pretty bad. Her clothes were torn and her eyes were puffy. Kisa needed a few minutes to catch her composure. Suddenly out of nowhere, Eisani jumped on Shea and began thumping on her and yelling, "You Fucking bitch! You almost had us killed, I should have beat your ass a long time ago."

Shea fell to the ground, crying and sobbing.

"Kisa why are you letting this happen? Please make them stop."

Sincere told Terry, "Break that shit up, man. Get E off of her. Butta, wake that nigga up and get this shit started."

Butta smacked Joe in his face a couple of times until he came around. When Joe woke up he was mumbling with blood and drool coming out of his mouth. "I'll give the paper back; just don't kill me! Please don't kill me?"

Sincere began laughing. "Damn, Joe, I thought you was such a big man. Pistol-whipped my wife while she was pregnant, and talked mad shit. Where is all that now, big man? I see you crying like a bitch now. I'm gonna let her pistol-whip your ass, and then I'm going to kill your ass. Now *that's* payback, and it's a muthafucka, ain't it? Here, Kisa, take this nine and handle your B I."

When he handed her the gun she felt something strange come down over her. She looked over her shoulder at Shea, who was staring at her, frozen in fear. Kisa shook her head and turned back to Joe. She tucked the gun in her waistband. She got real close to Joe's bloodied and battered face.

"Joe, just tell me what part Shea played in the setup and I won't let Sincere kill you."

"You promise?"

"I promise, sweetie, I have the gun right here."

Joe took a deep breath. Everyone in the room could see a deep relief come down over him.

"She gave us all the info on you and the operation. We plotted for a couple of days. She told us what night you would have the most money. She gave us a complete layout of your house and the shop.

"We were supposed to trap you off in the shop, but we were late. Shea was there and she watched the whole thing from the back of the Landcruiser. Kane, I'm sorry. Please forgive me. I was high on that dro and dust, I never meant to hit you like that. Plus I had been sniffing."

Kisa smiled with a deranged look in her eyes. "Oh, so now you crying like a bitch, coppin' pleas, snitching, and everything else." Kisa got closer to him and began talking louder with tears running down her face. "I didn't once beg your trifling, punk-ass for my life even with my child inside of me! *Did I?*" Kisa yelled so loud it was shrilling to everyone's ears; her face was streaked with black from her mascara and liquid eyeliner.

Sincere stepped up from behind her. "Kane, baby, give me the burner. That's enough."

Calmly but so cold she turned to him. "I'm not through yet."

The look in her eyes was so gone, he was scared to take the gun from her. But at the same time he was scared to let her keep it. He decided his best bet was to let her keep the gun and finish venting. For the next few minutes, Kisa felt as if she was outside of her body and watching her own actions. She pulled the gun from her waist, placed the muzzle on Joe's forehead, and asked him, "What's worst than death?"

Joe looked at her with a child-like look in his eyes. "Being tortured and suffering."

"Wrong!" Kisa yelled as she tapped his head with the gun. "Come on, what's the answer?"

"I don't know, Kane, please?" He begged.

She gave him an evil grin. "The only thing worse than death is the anticipation of death."

It was now becoming clear to everyone in the room that Kisa was going to try to kill him herself.

He looked in Kisa's eyes with that child-like expression on his face. "But, Kisa, you promised."

"Yeah, I promised. I promised that I wouldn't let Sincere kill you."

Joe began saying his Hail Mary's. Before he could complete it Kisa pulled the lever. It looked like his entire brain came out the back of his head. The sight of this made Eisani vomit. Kisa could have sworn he was still breathing. As a sign of disrespect, she placed the gun on his nose and blew the middle of his face off.

Now it would be impossible for him to have an open casket. Kisa took a deep breath, turned around, and looked at everyone; They were staring at the blood splattered all over her face and clothes, they were all shocked. She placed her eyes on Shea.

Kisa walked over to her and squatted down beside her. "Shea, you're my older sister, and regardless of anything, I will always love you. Now you know I'm not going to let anyone kill you. That's my word! I just need to know that you only told them to rob me, not to beat me while I carried your niece."

Shea began to speak, then she paused. She knew she might as well tell the truth. She half knew in her heart that Kisa wouldn't kill her; she would believe it wholeheartedly if she had not just seen her younger sibling kill a man. With a shaky voice Shea began to speak. "Kisa, I'm so sorry. I never thought they would hurt you. I got over my head in some money trouble with their crew. That's the only reason I went along with it. Keesy, you have to believe me. I'm truly sorry. You have to know I straight spazzed on him afterwards. Kisa, you have to know I love you so much."

Kisa had a look of forgiveness on her face; she wrapped her arms around Shea and squeezed her tight. Then, in an instant, she pushed her away and spat on her. "You are one pathetic bitch! You'll lie and attempt to slither your way out of anything you can, and it doesn't matter who you hurt. It wasn't about the money. How could you sit there and watch that faggot-ass nigga beat your younger sister while she was pregnant? And I really know it wasn't about no money trouble either, 'cause you could have come to me! I have never turned my back on you. It was just deeper than that; you have so much jealousy and larceny in your heart for me that I know you planned that entire thing. That's why I've hated and loathed you for the last five months. Now you're nothing to me. As a matter of fact, don't call our father anymore. You haven't spoken to him in three years, so don't start now. I don't ever want to see you in New York any more. If you see me, your best bet is to walk the other way. Don't ever cross me again, or the next time you *will* die! You fuckin' *bitch!*"

Kisa stood to her feet and kicked Shea in her face. "Get this bitch out of my sight."

Sincere walked over to her, took the gun out of her hand, and hugged her. "Baby, are you okay?"

"I'm aight. But Sin you have to promise me nothing will happen to her as long as my father is alive. And her mother too. You have to promise me that."

"I promise, Kisa, I will not kill her."

"Thank you, baby. Can you take Eisani and me to the house now? I need to get in the tub."

"Yeah, baby, go get in the truck; let me get these niggas squared away, and I'll be ready."

Kisa sat in silence and stared off into space as Sincere drove them home. She had already justified and came to terms with the homicide that she had just committed, chalking it all up: He tried to harm her child and her two cousins. Now that Kisa had her first murder under her belt, she now knew that she could and would kill for her family.

Sincere watched her. He made a note in his head to keep a close eye on her for a while. He had seen some of the hardest men go straight 7:30 after committing their first homicide.

Track 8: It Don't Get Mo Betta!

Life was getting normal again at least by Kisa's standards. Sincere had begun to run his business again. She now had more time for Kai, and it seemed like she had turned into the ghetto Martha Stewart. If Kisa had on a Coogi dress, Kai had on a Coogi sweater the same color. They even had matching Gucci hats.

Kisa took Kai on a slew of trips and shopping sprees like they were the same age. For two months straight, they were out of town visiting her relatives in the South and in Detroit.

Sincere quickly nipped that in the bud, telling Kisa, "You need to sit your ass still! I'm tired of coming home to an empty house every night."

At first she started to argue but decided against it. The entire time he was fussing, she was thinking to herself, *This nigga know he don't even come home at night let alone every night.*

The first couple of weeks that she and Kai were at home, she noticed a change in Sincere. He was spending a lot of time in the house and a lot of time with the baby. Kai was clearly becoming a daddy's girl. Kisa bought her more clothes than the average adult had and Sincere gave her enough jewelry to be a royal princess.

At six months, she had a pair of vvs-quality, H-color studs, a diamond nameplate, and a diamond bracelet. That was just the jewelry that Kisa let her wear daily. At her baptism, she wore a beautiful snow white Christian Dior gown, and Sincere had bought her a small platinum chain with a small diamond cross. Kai was definitely Harlem's little ghetto princess.

Kisa was even more amazed at how Sincere took Kai around with him everyday.

Kisa told Sincere, "You better not be taking my daughter around any business, and you better not be having no bitches around my daughter!"

Having Kai with him did attract a lot of extra attention. Every time females passed they commented on how gorgeous little Kai was. This was too much temptation for Sincere to get numbers, but he knew not to even play with Kisa like that.

As spring rose over the city, Kisa was getting her life on again. Lena was basically a live-in nanny, always taking Kai somewhere. Between her and Sincere, Kisa had to schedule time to spend with her own baby. With Sincere damn near never home again as it got warmer, and Lena as a live-in sitter, Kisa began going out with her cousins again. They were out drinking and clubbing. Kisa had really missed these days. Most nights it would just be her and Eisani.

One particular Wednesday night, she and Eisani went to the movies and then to Justin's for dinner and drinks. They really had no intentions on going clubbing, but everyone in Justin's seemed to be heading over to club Cheetah; it was Lenny the Barber's night.

"Come on, E, we should go," Kisa pleaded.

"Girl I'm not dressed."

"What is wrong with what you have on?" Kisa asked with a twisted look on her face.

"It's too plain."

"Chick, please. You have on Versace Couture from top to bottom; come on, we're going. Shit, look what I have on!" Kisa had on a ripped up Escada tee, a pair of ABS safety pin jeans, and BeBe spiked heel sandals. Even with this rough-sounding look, she appeared to just have stepped off the runway. After

Kisa begged and pleaded for another fifteen minutes, Eisani decided to go.

When they walked over to Cheetah's and saw the line, Kisa knew that there was no way she was standing in the line that was up the block. That's when she heard someone yelling out, "Yo, Kane!" She and Eisani turned around to see TaTa, Tyeise, and three other girls getting out of line walking towards them.

"What's up, ma?" Tyeise asked as she hugged her older cousins.

"Nothin', tryin' to see what's poppin' up in here."

TaTa, the original club hopper broke into the conversation. "Girl, you know this is a Lenny the Barber event; everybody be in here girl."

"You would know," Eisani hissed at her sister.

"Well, Kane, we know you not standing in line, so we rolling with you," Tyeis commented, standing in her very committed-around-the-way-girl-stance.

Kisa could only smile at her protégé.

"Come on then, silly."

Kisa quickly found herself a bouncer and handed him two crisp hundred-dollar bills to skip the line, and she told him she would give him another hundred if he could get them into VIP. And of course money always talks.

As soon as they sat down, drinks were ordered immediately. Kisa and Eisani, being the lushes they were, each ordered a bottle of Cristal. Within the next hour, the VIP was packed with the who's who of hip-hop: Jay-Z, with the entire Roc-A-Fella, Jermaine Dupri, Capone-n-Noreaga, Lil Cease, and the Junior Mafia, just to name a few.

Everyone knew who Kisa was, and they knew not to even try to fuck with her. No one, not even the hardest nigga, wanted that drama with her man.

Niggas couldn't help but drool over her with those tight ass jeans on, all tipsy and dancing around.

Her cousins were single, or at least not married, so they were getting their holla on. Kisa was winding and grinding to R. Kelly's *Fiesta* when she felt someone slip an arm around her waist and begin dancing with her.

Kisa did a one-eighty and came face to face with a drunken CoCo, who pulled her closer.

"Kane, I miss you so much. Please come home just for tonight ma. I need you."

Kisa was in a trance from his smell and how good he was looking. He had a fresh ceaser, and his goatee was trimmed just right. That only lasted for about five seconds.

"Boy, are you fucking crazy? Let me go. Half of fucking Harlem is in here what, you trying to get me killed?" Kisa pulled away and looked around. Everyone was staring. Those who didn't know Kisa were staring because they all wanted to know whom

Coco, was all up on like that. Kisa went to sit down. Coco followed her and sat next to her. "Ma, I'm sorry, but I'm serious, Kisa. I really need you. You know I would never do anything to get you hurt. I just need one night I want you to hold me."

"Coco, you are drunk. I'm not playing; get the fuck away. Not only is half of uptown in here, but the paparazzi is steady taking pictures of you. All I need is my man to open the fuckin' *Source* and see me next to you. Now go on somewhere."

CoCo stood up and began to walk away. He turned around. "You know I'm not giving up." He rejoined his entourage.

Eisani walked over to Kisa. "Now you know that did not look good."

"Imagine, if it didn't look good to you, how it looked to everyone else. And watch how they take it back to Sincere."

"Girl, don't worry about it. You know I'll vouch for you."

"Thanks, E. Can you find that waitress so I can order another bottle? That fucker done blew my high."

The family of girls continued to get their party on, not letting anything disturb their groove. Not even the grilling stares that Kisa was receiving from Coco.

When the club closed, everyone was standing outside for the let out. Kisa was ready to go, it was too many people outside, and then to top it off NYPD was trying to control the crowd but really making it worse.

"Yo, I'm not feeling this shit; it's too many motherfuckers out here who have not been searched, I'm ready to go."

"I'm feeling you, ma, and I'm leaving with you cause you know I don't do them hoes TaTa with."

Kisa, Tyeis, and Eisani headed for the Midnight Café. It was packed. They were able to get a seat after a short wait. They sat down and ordered their after-the-club-favorite turkey burgers and fries. Butta and Shawn walked over to the table.

"What's up, y'all?" Shawn asked, smiling like he'd won the lotto.

"What y'all doing out?" Kisa asked.

Butta bent down so only Kisa could hear him. "I saw that nigga, Coco, all up on you. Now I know you like a sister, so I'm not gonna say nothing to Sin, and Shawn didn't see it. But you know people gon' be telling. I'll cover for you if anything get back to Sincere, but tell that nigga to stay the fuck out your face before he get you and himself in trouble."

"Aight, Butta but you acting like I don't know. It won't happen again. That nigga was just pissy."

"Okay, lil' mama, but you know that nigga, Sin, get real jealous about any nigga he think in your face. You know ain't nothing worse than Coco to him."

"Where is Sin at anyway? He probably doing some shit he not supposed to be doing, and don't nobody ever tell on *his* ass!"

"I don't know where he is, he probably at home, he said he was going in early tonight. He was too tired to hang out."

"Oh well, whatever, Butta, I will see y'all around."

Butta walked to a table to join Shawn and the two girls, they had picked up at the club. The girl who was sitting next to Butta gave him a Who-the-fuck-was-that look, and she had the nerve to grill Kisa down.

Kisa shot her a look back that said, *Bitch don't even try me.*

Butta must have shut her down because her attitude changed immediately! Kisa ate her food quickly and was ready to be out. She thought to herself, *Too many muthafuckas in my business already.*

She waited for Tyeis and Eisani to finish eating. She paid the bill and was out.

On the way uptown to drop them off, Tyeis' cell phone rang. Ty was all giddy and happy, then she told whoever was on the other end to meet her at her house.

They dropped Eisani off at her building on 124th and Lennox, and shot over to 136th between Seventh and Eighth to drop Tyeis off. Kisa pulled up behind a familiar-looking Excursion.

"Ty, is this who you're meeting?"

"Yeah, you remember that rapper, Bless? Coco's artist. That's him."

Before Kisa could say anything, Coco was at her window.

"Coco, what is it?"

"*Damn.* Chill, ma. I just came to say my bad about that shit at the club. I was real high, and when I saw you dancing, I just acted out how I was feeling."

"Just don't do it no fucking more."

"But, Kane, I meant what I said. I need you. You the only one who understands me."

"Come on, Co, not this shit again; I got to go home, it's four-thirty."

Coco's eyes looked as if Kisa had crushed his world. She still had a weak spot for him. He was still her first love, and just smelling him made her panties damp. Smelling him reminded her of the nights they used to make love all night.

" Damn, Kane, I never thought you would turn on me like this. I just need to talk to you and for you to listen to me."

Kisa wrote down a number on a piece of paper. "Here is my cell number, call me only when you really need to talk or when it's really important." With that, Kisa handed him the paper, rolled up her window, and pulled off.

As Kisa pulled up to her house, she thought, *I am not getting out the bed until after 3:00 p.m.*

Sincere's Benz was in the driveway along with her truck and Lena's Q45, so she knew he had beaten her home for once.

After Kisa looked in on Kai, who was sleeping in her cradle, in the guestroom with Lena, she went to her bedroom. Sincere was snuggled up with the covers. He appeared to be knocked out.

Kisa undressed down to her underclothes, then quietly slid into the bed. As she got comfortable and closed her eyes she heard, "Where the fuck you been?"

She took a deep breath. "I been out."

" I know you been out. Where were you at?"

"I was at Cheetah's with my cousins."

"Oh so now you staying your ass out until dawn? You betta start actin' like you fucking married and bring your ass home at a decent time, I'm here waiting on you all night."

Kisa was tired, frustrated, and, now aggravated. "Nigga, don't start no shit with me cause you came home one night in twenty years."

"When I'm out all night, I'm working, not fucking whoring." Sincere never saw the smack coming, but he sure felt the sting.

Kisa jumped on top of him and started swinging and cursing. "Fuck you bastard. I give you any and everything you need. I've never cheated, while you are out there fucking everything moving, and you got the nerve to call me a whore. You the hoe, you fucking bitch. I hate you!"

Once Sincere got control of her swinging arms, he wrestled her down, but she wouldn't give up. They fell on the floor. He pinned her down and she was still trying to fight back. He grabbed her hair and smacked her with the back of his hand; Kisa tasted the blood in her mouth.

Lena opened the door and turned the light on. She was amazed at seeing how much shit they had knocked over in less than three minutes. Lena stared at them, almost naked, on the floor.

"I don't give a shit about this being your house. As long as this baby's here, ain't gonna be none of this shit. Now pull it together or I'll take her home to Harlem with me. And what the hell is wrong with ya'll, carrying on like savages at six in the morning."

Kisa stood up and grabbed a shirt.

When Lena saw Kisa's bloody lip she looked at Sincere. "I know I didn't raise dumb ass to be hitting on girls." She slammed the door and went back to her room.

Kisa grabbed a pillow and blanket off the floor and bumped past Sincere.

"Where the fuck you going?"

"Away from your ass," she hissed. Kisa went to the den and slept on the pullout couch.

For the next two weeks, Kisa and Sincere barely talked. If Sincere came home before Kisa went to bed, she would sleep in the den or a guest bedroom.

Sincere was getting tired of that shit, and he was about to go out of town to Miami for Memorial Day in two days. He left a note for Kisa to come to the city and meet him at Jimmy's for lunch. When Kisa arrived, they hugged and kissed for the first time in two weeks.

Sincere looked over at Kisa and smiled. "I know you still not mad at me."

"I'm not mad at nobody."

"I heard you was mad at Coco"

"Is that what you brought me here for? 'Cause I ain't for it; I can leave now."

"Nah, ma, I'm fucking with you. I just wanted to get everything straight before I leave for Miami."

Kisa smirked. "So when are y'all leaving?"

"Our plane is leaving Friday afternoon. You going to be aight wit me gone?"

"What are you talking about, Sin? We leaving Thursday!"

"And when were you going to tell me?"

"You never asked."

"Well I guess I'll let you go this time."

"*Let* me go? Nigga, *please!* I want you to start remembering you're my husband, and not my father."

"Aight, aight. I wanted you to come here so we could spend some time together peacefully. After this I want to go to the movies. I just want to hang out like we used to."

The young married couple enjoyed their time together. They even went home together by ten. They enjoyed watching movies and playing with Kai. They even made love, something Kisa missed dearly.

The next morning, everything was going great. Kisa got up and fixed breakfast. She heard her cell phone ringing upstairs. She didn't get there fast enough. She heard Sincere say "hello," then repeat it several times.

When she walked through the door, he threw the phone down.

"It must have been one of your lil' boyfriends. He got scared and hung up."

"No, whoever it was probably hung up because they thought they had the wrong number."

"Kisa, do you think I'm that stupid?"

"Whatever, Sincere. Breakfast is downstairs. I have to pack, my plane leaves in three hours."

While Kisa and Eisani sat waiting in the airport, her phone rang.

"Hello?"

"What's up, lil' mama?"

"Hi, Coco," Kisa spoke dryly.

Eisani looked over at her with raised eyebrows.

"*Damn.* Can you at least sound enthused to hear from me?"

"What do you need, Coco? I'm about to get on the plane."

"Where are you going?"

"To Miami"

"With your husband?"

"No, me and E"

"Yeah, me and my niggas gon' be there."

"I should have known."

"Well maybe I'll get to talk to you there, I called you earlier but Sincere answered."

"I should have known it was you, and no you can't talk to me in Miami cause Sin will be there."

"I hope we run into each other while we're down there."

"Whatever." And Kisa hung up.

Coco hung up smiling, knowing he had a full proof plan to bring Kisa back to him. And it would start this Memorial Day weekend.

Before Kisa could close her flip phone, Eisani was asking questions.

"Why is Coco calling you?"

"Girl, I don't even know. He swears he needs someone to talk to."

"Well I don't think you're the one, unless you really want Sincere to whip your ass."

Kisa let out a sigh. "Ma, let me do this, 'cause this is how I does it."

They both fell out in laughter at Kisa's comment. Then Eisani became serious. "Yeah, Elijah called me last night, telling me he was going to be in Miami, like I give a fuck."

"So whatever happened with that, E?"

"Ma, I had to let to that shit go. For real it was too much stress. The broad started calling me and shit, two-waying me. I just told him I couldn't do it anymore."

"Well how did he take that?"

"I guess he thought I was joking at first. He would call everyday for couple of weeks, you know, trying to make plans. After he saw that I was serious he left it alone. I get calls from him every now and then. He says he calls to see how I'm doing. What he really means is 'who are you fucking now?'"

Miami was all that. Kisa and Eisani stayed smoked out. During the day, they shopped, sunbathed at the beach, and walked the strip. They were happy, tanned, and glowing. They were attracting a lot of attention, especially on Saturday when Kisa wore her monogram Gucci bikini with the G's, and Eisani wore her Channel logo bathing suit with the C's. Everyone was on them, trying to holla.

Kisa's phone rang.

"Hello?"

"What hotel you staying in?" an angry voice asked.

"Who the fuck is this?"

"It's your husband! Oh, you don't know my voice now?"

"You sound all mad and shit. We're staying at the Ritz."

"Take your ass there now, change your clothes and I'm gonna meet you there."

"What?"

"You heard me! Go take that shit off! Niggas out here drooling over you! I see you!"

"Where you at, Sincere?" Kisa asked, looking around frantically.

"Don't worry about it. Do what I said."

"No."

"What do you mean? 'No!'"

"Exactly what I said. Shit, I'm at the fucking beach and this is what I wear at the beach. I paid twelve hundred dollars for this, and I'm gonna wear it."

"Kisa, I swear to God, if you don't take your ass to that hotel right now, I'm gonna embarrass your red ass right here on this strip!"

Kisa knew that he meant what he said, so she gave in. "Alright, I'll meet you there. *Damn.*"

When Kisa got to the hotel, Sincere, Butta, Shawn and Mannie were waiting in the lobby. Everyone went up to the suite. Eisani entertained everyone while Sincere and Kisa thumped it out in the bedroom. When Sincere walked out of the bedroom everyone knew he'd won the battle; he had the bikini in his hand.

"Come on, ya'll, let's go." He was smiling hard, even though Kisa had put fresh scratches on his face.

That night they ended up at the same club. When Kisa saw them she told Eisani, "Let's be out, because Sin all pissy and shit. I don't feel like dealing wit him."

"Okay, ma, just let me finish my drink and exchanging numbers with this nigga."

"Aight."

As they begin to exit the club, Kisa saw Sincere dancing with a well-built, thick chick dressed very skimpy in a mini skirt that barely covered her ass. Sincere was in a drunken stupor, with one hand all on her ass, and a half-empty Belvedere bottle in the other.

As Kisa got closer, she noticed the chick had her hands down the front of his pants.

Sincere had no clue-that Kisa was even in the club. Really he was too drunk to even notice.

Kisa walked up and stood right behind him. She stared at the girl's smiling face and realized that she knew this bitch. Her name was Milani, from a dozen Rap and R&B videos.

Shawn, Mannie and Butta saw her, but they were so high and drunk, they found the shit amusing, and couldn't warn Sincere in time.

Kisa calmly tapped him on his shoulder. He turned around. He was so drunk, it took a few seconds to register that it was his wife.

Kisa didn't give him time to say a word before she began thumping on him.

Milani didn't want no part of this crazy bitch standing in front of her; she got the hell up out of there, but not before giving Shawn her number so he could give it to Sincere.

Kisa kept hitting him until she felt like stopping, and he was too drunk to defend himself. All he could do was yell at Kisa.

"Go on, Kisa, stop playing and shit. What the fuck is wrong with you? You bugging."

When the bouncers walked over, she removed herself voluntarily without them asking her. Kisa and Eisani walked to the parking lot. Kisa wanted to break down and cry, but pride wouldn't let her. Eisani wanted to reach out to her cousin but knew it was better to let Kisa talk when she was ready. As they walked, a cream and beige Bentley inched up beside them. Kisa clearly had an attitude and did not feel like being harassed by any nigga; until she heard his voice.

"Kisa Kane and E, ya'll need a ride? It ain't safe for you ladies to be out late like this."

Kisa cracked a grin. "I sure do."

Eisani pulled her to the side. "Look, Kisa, I know you're upset about this shit you just went through tonight, and the shit ya'll have been going through back home. But do you think this is a good idea?"

"Fuck Sin! And why the fuck is everyone so concerned about him all the time. What about me?" Kisa began to cry.

Eisani reached out to hug her, but Kisa pulled away.

"No, E, that's okay. Here are the keys to the rental car. I'm going with Coco. I'll have him bring me back shortly. I'll be okay. You be safe. I'm turning my phone off, but I will be checking my messages. So if you need me, leave a message. See you later."

"Bye, girl."

Once Eisani got back in the room, she was glad that the night had ended early. She was exhausted. She checked her voicemail. She had ten new messages. Five of them were from guys whom she had met at the beach; two messages were from TaTa, and two were from her mother. The last one was from Elijah.

"...What up boo I was calling to check on you see how everything was going. I also wanted to know if you wanted to hang out with me tonight. So if you get this message by twelve-thirty give me a call, if I don't hear from you by then I will go ahead to South beach with my mans and them..."

Part of her wished she had gotten the message in time. She still loved him and longed for him. But the other part was glad she'd missed the call. The more she didn't have to see him, the quicker she could get over her feelings for him. She put on her pajamas and rolled up some hydro.

Eisani took a couple of puffs and put it out. It was some potent dro. The combination of the weed and her fatigue put her in a very deep sleep. Thirty minutes later Eisani was awakened, by loud knocking.

"Who?"

"Sincere. Open the door."

Eisani opened the door and let him in.

"Kane is not here."

"Where the fuck is she?"

Sincere was a lot more sober than he was an hour ago.

"I don't know. Shit, you pissed her off so bad she don't even wanna talk to me. She said she needed time to be alone."

"Well I'll just wait here for her. As a matter of fact, I'm going to lay in her bed."

"Suit yourself. I'm going back to my room and my sleep. When Kane comes back, please don't be up in here disturbing the peace, fighting and shit." Eisani went in the room; slamming the door behind her, just knowing it was about to be some shit.

As soon as Sincere hit the bed he was out.

Kisa was enjoying drinks and memories with Coco at his waterfront condo. Coco was able to vent his frustrations and problems about the record industry and things in his personal life. Kisa listened and gave him honest advice. They talked and laughed until it was almost sunrise.

"Co, I think you need to take me back to the Sheraton. I think we will be too noticeable in the daylight."

"Okay ma. You know that's not a problem, even though you could stay here with me"

"Come on Coco, we had such a good time. Don't ruin it."

"I'm just playing with you, shorty. Let me get my keys and I'll be ready."

Kisa had promised Coco that she would keep in touch and not be so disgruntled towards him anymore. When she got upstairs and saw Sincere sound asleep in her bed she thought to herself, *I should have known.*

She was saddened just looking at him, thinking about how much she loved him but yet all the shit he'd put her through. The tears began to bubble in her eyes. She couldn't fight them. She decided to just take a hot shower. She let the water hit her for thirty minutes, while she let all her tears out.

When she stepped out of the shower, Sincere was sitting on top of the toilet.

"Look, Sincere, I don't feel like it right now. I'm tired, I want to go to sleep before our flight leaves tonight."

"Kisa, I didn't come here to fight. I came to apologize, I know I was dead wrong. Ma, I was pissy-pissy. I really wasn't in my right mind. You know I don't even get down like that. You know all the shit I'm going through back home. The streets and all the stress they give me. I mean I just felt so relaxed down here. And I was pissy and high, just too relaxed, not in my right state of mind. Ma, I need you to understand."

"Are you finished?"

"What you mean, *am I finished?* You don't have anything to say?" Sincere asked with a bewildered look on his face."

"Sin, I told you I don't want to talk about it right now."

"That's the problem now, you don't ever wanna talk about shit. Well your ass ain't leaving out this bathroom until we talk." Sincere locked the door and stood in front of it.

Kisa sat on the edge of tub, crossed her legs, and folded her arms. They sat in silence for more than ten minutes. He knew she could play this game all day. She was as stubborn as a mule.

After fifteen minutes he said, "Fuck it. You can go on. I'm going to take a shower." He unlocked the door and Kisa went to bed in the nude just to mess with his head, because she had no plans of giving him any.

Sincere took a long hot shower. For the first time, he clearly thought about what had happened the night before and how badly Kisa was probably hurting. But as bad as he was feeling right now, he was still looking forward to his date with Milani tonight. Kisa and Eisani would be back in New York tonight, so he planned for everything to be drama-free.

Sincere slid into bed, wrapped his arm around Kisa's body, and pulled her close. Kisa tried to pull away, but his hold was too strong. When he flipped her over, her face was streaked with tears.

"Ma, please stop crying. I can't take us being like this anymore."

He began to kiss her; she couldn't fight him anymore. They both cried as they made love. Kisa cried because she loved him so much, but hated him at the same time. She hated him because she would never be able to get away from him; his hold was too strong. He cried because when she hurt he really did hurt too. Even though he would go out and do the same thing again tomorrow. They fell asleep wrapped inside of one another.

Eisani and Kisa returned home that night. Kisa was glad to be home with Kai. She put Kai in the bed with her that night. Kisa sat up, watching TV, thinking how this time she was going to get back at Sincere. Kisa was thinking, He needs an eye opener to see that I will leave his ass.

Her cell phone rang, breaking her train of thought. "Yeah"

"I heard you left Miami already."

"Hi, Coco. What's up?"

"Nothing, baby. I wanted to see if we could have a private dinner at my place. But you left without saying goodbye."

"Boy, you don't be listening. I told you my plane was leaving tonight."

"So how was your stay?"

"Besides Sincere making part of it hell, Eisani and I had plenty of fun."

"Well next time you're down, maybe y'all can stay at my crib."

"Maybe. We'll have to see."

Coco couldn't believe the response he'd gotten from Kisa. He knew now that he was getting closer than ever. He knew that it was because of her and

Sincere's problems, but he would take her any way he could get her.

"Well, Kane, I hope you are serious about that 'maybe.'"

"I am. Look, I'm laying here with Kai; she is sleep and I'm dead-tired, so hit me tomorrow."

"I'll be back in the city tomorrow, so if you're free, maybe we can spend some time together."

"Sure, just call me around five or six, okay?"

"That's a bet lil' mama, I'll holla later."

"One." After Kisa hung up she felt a sense of relief, thinking to herself, *this is some dangerous shit I'm on right now. The danger is always what makes it exciting though.*

When Sincere returned, he gave Kisa her space and let her do her thing. He didn't badger her about her whereabouts or her comings and goings. He decided to let her live her life. He was concerned about her cheating out of revenge. But he was so cocky about her position in his life, he knew with all his heart that she would never cheat on him.

He didn't have much time to sweat her activities. His business and his new mistress took a good bit of his time. Milani was his new side activity since they'd returned from Miami. He began buying her expensive gifts, taking her on dates and trips. He always took care of any woman he dealt with. His train of thought was, *it ain't tricking if you got it.*

Kisa didn't really pay him much attention either; she was having too much fun with Coco, even taking Kai with her sometimes. Her and Coco's visits were usually at his home or somewhere very private, to keep pictures from being taken by the paparazzi, or anyone seeing them.

They were not having sex but had kissed once. Kisa had not let it go any further. Coco showered her and Kai with gifts that they didn't need. Most of all, Kisa really enjoyed his companionship. She was really happy once again, riding around in her big six, daughter in tow, thinking, *Life: it don't get mo betta!*

Track 9: That's That Shit

Sincere had been seeing Milani for only three months but had grown tired of her already. To him the girl was crazy. She would call him day and night. She would cry when he wouldn't come to see her, and she would even go without eating for days.

Sincere tried to talk to her because he wanted to keep her around. The girl was a real freak. But she would not cooperate with the program.

One weekend, Sincere and Kisa flew to Vegas for the Zab Judah fight. On their first day there, Milani called Sincere's phone all day back to back. He finally answered while Kisa was shopping, and he answered very disgruntled. "What the fuck do you want?"

That didn't even phase her simple ass. "Sincere, where are you?"

"I am out of town with my wife!"

"Oh, so you are with her."

He could tell that she was crying and pouting, because it made her Brazilian accent very strong. Sincere inhaled deeply before he spoke. "And what do you mean by that? Yeah, I'm with Kane; she's my wife."

"What about me, Sincere? I need you. I can't eat or sleep."

Sincere could not believe what he was hearing. "Look bitch, you knew from the door I had a wife. And I am not mistreating her or leaving her for no bitch. As a matter fact, your crazy ass can lose my number. I don't want to ever see your psychotic ass again; that's my word." Sincere terminated the call and cut the phone off.

Kisa was inside the Gucci boutique, but she had been watching him. She could see that whomever he was talking to was making him very upset. When the saleslady came back with Kisa's change and her purchase, she left the store and walked over to him. "Who were you talking to?"

"Nobody!" he answered harshly.

"It had to be somebody I could tell from the store you were extremely upset. Oh my bad it must have been one of your bitches."

Sincere didn't even entertain Kisa's comment.

"Whatever, ma. Did you get my sweater and pants?"

"Yes," Kisa responded with an attitude.

"Did you find something nice to wear to the fight?" Sincere asked, trying to change the conversation to one of Kisa's favorite subjects.

"Yes I did," Kisa towards the next store.

Sincere had to leave his phone off the rest of the trip. He had no other choice. Every time it rang and he didn't answer, Kisa gave him dirty looks.

When they returned to New York, Kisa could see that Sincere was experiencing another one of his come-home-early-and-stay-in-the-house-phases. He even had Shawn, Mannie, and Butta hanging with him around the house.

He had completely cut Milani off, which turned her into a stalker. She called all day and all night; she even called the house once. Sincere felt lucky he was home alone that day and that he had answered the phone. He changed the number immediately. He told Kisa that he'd changed the number because he thought it was tapped.

Milani would come to wherever she thought Sincere would be. Often he had to embarrass her. Once, she was so hysterical he smacked her. He could not understand how a woman so beautiful could be so crazy. He figured, *Shit she could have any man she wants. Why does she make a fool of herself chasing me down?*

He just chalked it up that *the bitch is disturbed, plain and simple.* After he'd cut her off, he decided he was not going to mess around with anyone else. He tried to make it all about Kisa. But the more time he spent in the house, the more he noticed that Kisa wasn't there much any more. And she was happy about something that he could not put his finger on.

Kisa still wasn't paying him any attention. She was living her life again. Tyeis was in a serious relationship with Bless now. They practically lived together when he wasn't on the road.

Coco would fly Kisa, Tyeis and Eisani out to parties or anywhere they were performing. Kisa went with him out of town to business meetings and to the studio, and they all spent weekends at his summer rental home in the Hamptons.

Coco was happy to have Kisa back in his life, right by his side. Even though their relationship was secret and, so far, nonsexual, he enjoyed every moment. In his scheming mind he knew if he played his cards right, she would come around.

Two days after returning from Vegas, Kisa and Eisani drove to Demetria's house in North Carolina. When they pulled up to the house, Demetria was in the yard working in her garden. She stopped to see who was in her driveway, a big smile spread across her face. Kisa hopped out the car and embraced her mother.

"Hi, Mommy."

"Hi, baby. What are you doing here?"

"Well I'm going to Miami tomorrow, so I brought Kai down here instead of leaving her with Lena. I thought you might want to keep her for a couple of days."

"Yes, I want to keep my baby. I don't get to see her as it is."

Eisani took Kai out of her car seat and walked over to Kisa and Demetria. "Hi Auntie."

"Hey, Eisani. Come give me a hug. And where is your mother; why didn't she come down?"

"We decided to drive down yesterday. She said she couldn't get off on such short notice."

"Your mother is a trip. She could have gotten off. Shit, she don't even have to work, all that money your daddy left her."

"Auntie, you know she tight."

"Trust me, I know! Hand me my grandbaby."

Demetria took Kai into her arms and hugged her as if she had not seen her in years. She planted kisses all over her face. "Hey my precious baby. How are you? I bet you don't even know who I am; they hardly bring you to see me. You probably think Lena is your only grandmother."

Kisa interrupted her mother's doting. "Ma, come on with all that. We were just here a month ago. Anyway, you could come up top more often."

"Girl, shut up and come on in this house. Let me give you a list of things to get from the store for the dinner tonight."

Kisa frowned like a little kid and started whining. "But, ma, I'm tired. You always putting somebody to work, like grandma."

Demetria prepared a feast and invited all of Kisa's aunts, uncles, and cousins over. Everyone sat around, ate, drank, and conversed all night. They told stories about Kisa and Eisani when they were younger. Their drunken uncle, who was barely able to sit up in the chair, began speaking with a slurred speech.

"Oh, them two there. Shit, one in the north and one in the south. But when they came together they was hell on wheels. Sneaking out of Big Mama's house to go to the club, smoking weed, and getting arrested for assault. The two of you was a something else; I swear."

Kisa and Eisani were tired of all the stories of how bad they were. Demetria was getting tired of it too. Her oldest brother, James, and sister, Ann, loved to sit around and talk about other people's children. They acted like their kids were angels.

Demetria could admit that while Kisa and Eisani were running wild, James and Ann's kids were into the church, volunteer groups, and on the honor roll. That was then. Now, both their sons were strung out on dope. Both of James's daughters had three kids with three different daddies. Both were on welfare and not trying to better themselves in any way.

Ann's daughters dumped their kids off on her and turned into local porno stars. If Eisani's mother, Maria, had been there, she would have cursed them out and sent them on their way. Demtria decided that since her little sister was absent, she would politely send them off.

"Well, my baby and Eisani most certainly turned into two responsible adults with their own businesses. They both lead exotic and comfortable life styles. Speaking of exotic, we have to send y'all home now so we can clean up. I have to get up and take the girls to the airport in the morning. They're flying to Miami."

Everyone said their good byes as they left. Once Demetria shut the door, Kisa exhaled and looked at her mother and Eisani. "I'm so glad that damn Anne and James is gone. Everybody else could have stayed, but them two, they be over doing it."

"I know," Eisani agreed.

"Well, you two go in there and get that kitchen clean for me, and I will put Kai to bed."

Eisani began clearing the dining room table as Kisa followed Demetria into the bedroom.

"Mommy, you don't have to worry about taking us in the morning. I called a car service. And if Sin happens to call here while we're gone just tell him we rode down to Myrtle Beach with LaQuan for a concert."

"Now, Kisa, why are you lying to your husband?"

"No reason. I just wanted to get away for a while."

"Girl, don't lie to me. You know Lena and I talk everyday. She told me that you and Sincere been acting real funny with each other lately. Now what is that about?"

"Its not about nothing, Ma. We're just going through something right now. Personally, I'm just going through the valley of indecision right now, and I need my space."

"Only thing the two of you are going through right now is letting the streets, or better yet, you're still letting that street shit run your lives."

"Mommy, that is nonsense. I don't even want to discuss it anymore. I'm going to bed. I'll wake you in the morning before we leave."

She kissed her mother goodnight and went into her old bedroom. She lay awake most of the night, thinking of her mother's words. They hurt her because she knew they were true. She tossed and turned so much, by the time she fell asleep the alarm was going off.

When Kisa and Eisani got off the plane in Miami, it was hot, scorching deep-south hot the kind of heat that takes your breath away. Once inside the air-conditioned airport, they could breathe again. Kisa looked for CoCo at the baggage claim where they were supposed to meet. "Where is he? It is too hot down here. I'm ready to shower and change clothes." Kisa felt someone tap her on the shoulder. She turned around to face a tall, brown skin man dressed in a dark suit and hat.

"Are you Mrs. Montega?"

Kisa looked him up and down then replied, "That depends on who you are."

"I'm sorry, ma'am, allow me to introduce myself. I'm Gerald, CoCo's driver. He sent me to pick you up."

"And where is he?"

"He was called away on emergency business. He told me to take you where ever you wanted to go."

"I just want to go to his house for now. And when will he be back?"

"Late tonight or early in the morning."

Kisa and Eisani had hung out all day in Miami, just sight seeing. Kisa repeatedly called CoCo's cell phone. Each time she called, she got his voice mail. She was disappointed. She felt like he was ducking her.

That night, she and Eisani found a nice little club to party at in South Beach. It was mainly filled with locals. They were having fun but it really wasn't their speed. The DJ was playing nothing but bounce music, so they turned in early.

Back at Coco's house, they sat around the pool and smoked blunts. Eisani swam laps while Kisa sat on the edge with her feet in the water. It was a beautiful night. A full moon and the stars were out. Kisa sat, gazing up at the sky. Her cell phone rang, scaring her half to death. She looked at the caller ID and saw that it was Coco she answered with an attitude. "Where the fuck you at?"

Coco knew she would be mad. He took a deep breath. "Whoa. Slow down, ma. I'm out in Cali."

"You with a broad or something?"

"No!"

"Well why weren't you answering my phone calls?"

He smiled at the thought that she may be jealous. "I'm not answering my personal line. Why didn't you call my business number?"

"I didn't know I was supposed to! Why in the hell didn't you call me before I flew all the way down here?"

"This business came up two hours before your plane landed. I swear I'll make it up to you tomorrow when I get back."

"What time you will you be back?"

"Sometime in the afternoon."

"Well, you know my plane leaves Sunday morning."

"You can stay longer, Kane."

"No, I have to get back to Charlotte, pick up Kai, and drive back to New York."

"What are y'all doing now?"

"We're in your pool."

"I wish I was there."

"I bet you do. Well it was nice to finally hear from you. See you tomorrow I'm going to bed. Goodnight."

"Good night."

In was a rainy Wednesday. Sincere had grown restless with Kisa being gone so much. He decided to approach her with caution. Everyone was home so Kisa cooked Dinner. During dinner, he watched Kisa feeding Kai and talking with Lena. He was pretty quiet trying to figure out how he was going to approach Kisa without starting a war.

Once everyone was finished, Lena cleared the table while Kisa bathed Kai and put her to bed. Kisa joined Lena and Sincere in the den where they were watching *Love and Basketball* on DVD. She didn't even bother to sit next to Sincere on the couch, which is where she usually sat when they watched movies. Lena could feel the tension, so she told them, "I'm going to turn it in now; this rain is making me tired. So goodnight and y'all need to fix whatever is going on between you two."

She walked up the stairs without even giving them a chance to respond.

After ten minutes, Kisa decided to go clean the kitchen, she could no longer concentrate on the movie.

When she walked by Sincere, he thought, *Damn she looks so sexy in that tank top and them cut off jeans.*

Then he tried to remember the last time they had had sex. He waited for about twenty minutes before he went into the kitchen. He knew it didn't take long for Kisa to wash dishes. He walked up behind her, hugged her, and kissed her neck. She just kept washing dishes, trying to ignore him. So he stepped back and decided to get to the matter at hand.

"Kisa, you been gone too much again. Don't you think you need to give it a rest?"

She turned around and looked at him like he was stupid. "Sincere, don't start that shit with me again, okay? Just cause all of sudden you want to be in the house."

"You need to start actin' like my wife and Kai's mother! Stop running the streets giving away my shit!"

"What shit?"

"That Shit between your legs, and don't lie and say you not fucking no one else, 'cause you not fucking me!"

"So that means I have to be fucking someone? Well if *you* not fucking me, then who *are* you fucking, Sin? Cause I don't see you running around here begging me for some. So you wanna fuck? Come on, let's go upstairs. We can fuck all night!"

He just stared at her and shook his head, knowing she was being sarcastic.

He told her, "You gonna make me choke the shit out of your ass in here"

"Fuck you, Sincere! I'm not even entertaining you tonight I'm going to bed."

He blocked her so she couldn't get by. "It must be your new nigga got you acting like this. But you better know this: When I find out who he is I'm gonna put some heat in both y'all asses."

She looked him right in the eye and said, "Whatever, Sin, that's your guilty mind fucking with you, 'cause you was fucking with that video ho!"

He squinted his eyes but said nothing.

"Oh pick your face up off the floor I bet you didn't think I knew about that one. I had been knew about you and that bitch. You can't even be discreet with your shit. And you telling me to act like your wife? Act like a husband. And how many wives do you know would run their husband's cocaine business while he was locked up, and then stay with him while he made her look foolish? You got all these bum-ass bitches that, if you put them all together, ain't half the woman I am! All of them out here laughing at me. So before you go complaining about the way my shit smell, sniff your own, with your bitch ass. I hate you."

Kisa stomped off pushing him aside.

Sincere stood in shock at how well Kisa knew him. It *was* his guilt that caused him to accuse her. He truly knew nothing about her and Coco.

Sincere pulled out a bottle of Belvedere and decided to go finish the movie. Kisa sat on the bed and rolled a blunt filled with chocolate and dro to prepare for round two; she knew he wasn't going to give up so easy. While she waited for the blunt to dry, she went downstairs to get a couple of Heinekens.

Sincere heard her in the kitchen and called her. "Yo, Kane, come here, baby."

She could tell he was drinking, so she ignored him and went back upstairs. She sat on the edge of the bed and began to smoke. She finished one Heineken and started on her second. She put the blunt out after smoking half of it. She was too high to even move, she finished her second beer and decided to watch a rerun of the *X-files,* hoping Sincere would not interrupt.

As soon as she got into the story, Sincere came in and turned it off.

"What the fuck did you do that for?"

"Why didn't you come see what I wanted when I called you?"

"Are you going to talk my head off with this bullshit all night? Let me know so I can go downstairs and sleep."

Kisa motioned to walk past him. He blocked her way, which began a light-shoving match.

"Come on, Sin.   For real I don't need this tonight."

He pushed Kisa down onto the bed and laid on top of her.

"Kisa, I love you and only you, none of those other bitches ever meant anything to me. I don't even fuck with nobody else now and never will again. I only want and need you, but you making this shit hard on a nigga." He began kissing her. At first she fought it, then she just gave in. He ripped her tank top in two and yanked her shorts off. They didn't make love that night, they fucked, and it was hard, almost violent. It seemed as if they were fighting, fighting for control.

After they finished, Kisa took a long hot shower.

When Kisa came out of the bathroom, Sincere asked her, "Why did you shower? Like I'm some nigga in the street."

She continued putting lotion on her body and putting on her pajamas. Sincere was getting aggravated. "So you still iggin me?"

Kisa got in the bed and told him, "Look, I gave you what you wanted so can you just let a bitch be. I just want to go to sleep. We can talk all day tomorrow."

So Sincere let it go and went to sleep.

Milani had just left Kisa's hair salon on 125th street. She had broken into the salon and completely trashed everything on the inside. She put horse manure in all of the chairs, and left dead squirrels on all the booths. She spray-painted the walls. They read *Sincere and Milani Forever.* On her way out she busted out all of the windows.

When she got to Sincere and Kisa's house she pulled out a black duffel bag containing red liquid paint, red spray paint, and black spray paint. She poured the red liquid paint all over Kisa's white Benz, and spray-painted in black letters *Sincere is mine BITCH.*

Then she spray-painted, in white letters, all over Sincere's black Benz, *Sin and Milani Always.* She even went as far to spray-paint the front of the house with hearts. And on the front door she wrote Sincere a letter:

Baby, I need you. Please come home. That bitch can't love you like I can! XOXO Milani.

The next morning, Kisa woke up with a headache. She gently slid from beneath Sincere's arm and got out of the bed.

She threw on a sweat suit so she could go to the store. When she got downstairs Lena was feeding Kai.

"Good morning, Mommy, good morning, Madison Kai Montega! Did you sleep good? Give me a big hug and all your sugar."

Kai just giggled as Kisa continued to play with her.

"Mommy has to go get something for this headache. I'll take you to the city today and we can go to the park and play. Then we can go to FAO Shwartz."

"Does that headache have anything to do with all that arguing you and Sincere were doing last night?"

"No, Mommy, it's not that serious."

"Well the two of you have certainly changed towards one another, and I don't like the way you are acting with this child here in the house."

"I think we worked it out, Mommy."

"Well if you did that's good; you need to keep your family together. Don't let all that shit in the streets come and interrupt your home life. Do you see what I'm getting at? Because I see all the tit for tat games you and Sincere are playing, one trying to see who can hurt who more. And I know that's probably not how it started out, especially on your part, but that's what it has turned into."

Kisa sat and took in everything Lena said.   "I understand, Mommy."

"And don't think I am just getting on you, I'll talk to Sincere too when he gets out the bed. I won't hold you up any longer. And can you bring some milk; this is Kai's last bottle."

"Now, Mommy, why you saying that like that ain't my daughter? Do you need anything else from the store?"

"Yeah bring me some ginger ale."

Kisa did not even bother to take her doobie pins out. Since they had been living in Jersey anytime she went out the house she took her pins out. It wasn't like living in Harlem, where some days she would leave her hair pinned all day.

When Kisa opened the front door, she damn near passed out. She walked towards the cars for a closer look. She was getting ready to let Sincere have it. As she turned around to go back in the house, she saw what Milani had done to the house "What the Fuck!" She began yelling for Sincere at the top of her lungs. "Sincere, get your ass out that fucking bed and get down here, now!"

She kept yelling until he appeared at the top of the stairs and Lena came from the kitchen holding Kai.

"Kisa, baby, what is the fuss about?" Lena asked.

"Ask your son, and just look what his other bitch did to the cars and our house."

Sincere could not believe what he was seeing; he began mumbling to himself. "Fucking bitch; I'm going to kill her ass."

Kisa just rolled her eyes at him. "Oh, so now you want to kill her? Please! Spare me! I'm moving back to Harlem and I'm taking Kai with me! I can't stand your ass. I can't stand to be around you. You just fucking disgust me, plain and simple! Lena I'm going to get the milk; I'll be right back."

Kisa hopped in her Range Rover and sped off. Lena just looked at her son and shook her head. "You gonna lose a good woman all because you can't keep your dick inside your pants." Lena pushed past Sincere and walked in the house.

On the way to the store, Kisa called Eisani, and Eisani called TaTa on three-way. Kisa told them the entire story, starting from the night before with she and Sincere's fight. She was still talking to them while she was driving from the store when Tyeis called.

"Hold on, y'all, Ty is on the other line." Kisa clicked over. "Hello?"

"Yo, Kane, somebody has trashed the shop and spray painted the walls with some shit about Milani and Sin." Tyeis sounded hysterical and confused at the same time. "I probably forgot to set the alarm again.

"Its okay, Ty, I know who did it. She paid a visit to my house too. I'm talking to E and Ta now. I'll be in the city when I get dressed and packed up."

"Do you want me to call the police?"

"Yeah, you can. I'll need a report for the insurance company."

"Aight then. One."

"One."

Kisa clicked back over to Eisani and TaTa. "That was Ty. She said that bitch fucked up my salon too!"

Eisani was ready to ride for her cousin. She was heated. TaTa had to ask the logical questions. "Kisa you think she got to the day spa?"

"Ma, I don't even know. I doubt it, though, 'cause don't too many people know I own it. Well look, I just pulled up to the house. Ya'll just be ready cause we're going to get this bitch. One."

Kisa looked at her house and began crying. She walked through the door and sat the groceries down in the foyer. Lena walked out of the den and met Kisa as she walked towards the stairs.

"Baby, stop crying. You can't let this get you down. Remember what we just talked about."

"It's not that, Mommy. That trifling bitch trashed my salon. He's going to give me her address so I can kill her."

As soon as Kisa got upstairs, she began verbally attacking Sincere. He just continued to get dressed, not saying anything in his own defense. He knew there was no use. She was too mad and was not trying to hear anything he had to say.

After she finished saying what she had to say and packing her clothes, she began Kai's clothes. She didn't say anything else to Sincere. Not even when he told her, "You don't have to leave, I can go stay with Butta." She just continued packing, totally ignoring him. He was too happy when he heard the sound of Butta's horn blowing outside. He told Kisa, "I'll be back later so we can talk when you calm down some. At least stay until I get back."

On his way out, Kai was sitting on Lena's lap.

"Give daddy a hug. I love you, baby girl. See you when I get back. Bye, Mommy."

He bent down to kiss Lena on her cheek and she turned her head.

"Go on, Sincere. I'm too disappointed with you right now."

That really hurt Sincere. He walked out of the house.

Once inside the truck with Butta, he had to hear it from him too.

"I told you not to fuck with that crazy girl. You don't listen. You think I just be trying to hate because Kisa and me are close. Then you want to let Mannie and Shawn boost you up to mess with these hoes. 'Cause they don't know shit about having a committed relationship and someone to love them. Nigga, you need to remember, misery loves company. And now that bitch has really created chaos in your life. That's that shit."

Sincere sighed, "Oh not you too. First Mommy, now you. Come on already, I feel like shit and my head hurt."

"Say no more, my man, but I'm surprised Kane ain't kill your simple ass."

"Man, I thought she was. And on top of that, the crazy bitch trashed Kane's salon."

"Say word!"

"Word. And Kane already said her and Kai is moving back to Esplanade."

Sincere and Butta rode around all day looking for Milani, they couldn't find her anywhere; it seemed as if she had disappeared.

When Sincere and Butta returned to the house, Kisa and Kai were gone. Kisa didn't leave a note, but Lena left him one, letting him know she would be at her own apartment in Harlem, and she would have Kai with her, so he could come by there to see her.

She also let him know that she wanted to talk to him. Sincere called Kisa at Esplanade, on her cell, and paged her. No luck.

Kisa didn't want to work this one out. If she ever needed CoCo, she needed him now. She went to his house that night. She had left Kai with Lena. She told Lena. "I'm going out of town to clear my head. And that's all Sincere needs to know."

When Kisa got to Coco's house, he soothed and comforted her. If Kisa ever needed any motivation to sleep with Coco, she had it now. Even when Coco had had next to nothing he could be the most romantic person in the world. His plan to get Kisa in his arms worked better than he thought. He had paid Milani two thousand dollars just to push up on Sincere, and to keep him away from Kisa so he could get next to her again.

He didn't know that the psychotic bitch would fall in love with Sincere and take the issue so far. CoCo was happy about it though. This was the most vulnerable he had ever seen Kisa.

They had dinner in his bedroom. After dinner, he put on one of Kisa's favorite CDs, Faith Evans. He told her, "I just wanna dance for a while."

Kisa leaned on him for support, physically and mentally. She just let him lead as she rested her head on his shoulder. When *Caramel Kisses* came on, Kisa squeezed Coco tighter, and sang along with Faith. This was her testament to him for being there for her in her time of need.

...*Caramel kisses you send my way. I won't complain, boy, don't go away...*

After Faith's CD had ended, Coco had all of their old favorite slow songs programmed to play starting with R. Kelly's *Your Body Is Calling*. When she heard it, she looked at him and smiled. "You don't forget anything, do you?"

"I'll never forget you or anything about you. I swear I'll never stop loving you I don't care whose wife you are. You will always be mine."

He rubbed her face and began to kiss her ever so passionately. He undressed her slowly and laid her down on the floor. He handled her like she was fragile glass. He poured Cristal over her bare breasts and began to lick it off it slowly.

For hours, CoCo made love to Kisa. She loved the way he took his time. Even during quickies, he never rushed her or went too fast. After they climaxed for the last time, he picked her up and led her to the bed.

He laid her down and held her while she slept. For the next four days, Coco took care of Kisa the best way he knew how. It only took a second for him to figure out what she needed.

At first he thought about taking her away. But there wasn't a place she had not been. And no shopping spree she had never experienced. So he decided to give her what she needed the most; time and attention.

CoCo canceled all his plans and business meetings, and stayed secluded in the house with her. They watched movies, listened to CD's, and just talked. Kisa was so happy, but at night she felt sad over her relationship with Sincere. She never imagined it would come to this. Not in a million years could she have envisioned cheating on the love of her life.

Everyday, when she called to check on Kai, Lena would try to talk to her about Sincere.

She would tell her, "He is hurting Kisa, he is sorry about the entire situation. And, baby, he's so worried and he doesn't like not knowing where you are."

Kisa calmly told Lena, "No disrespect to you mommy, because I know you mean well by talking to me. But Sincere should be hurting, and he can't possibly be hurting as bad as me. And as far as that sorry shit, that is exactly what he is, *sorry!*"

Lena did not stress her anymore about the issue, she knew her son was dead wrong.

Kisa had finally found peace of mind, which made her feel uneasy. She could feel it in the air; something was about to go down.

Track 10: No More Drama

Friday was a cool, somber day. Kisa had been at Coco's house for a week and a half now. She was preparing to up Kai up on Saturday and take her down south for a couple of weeks.

Sincere had given up on calling her cell phone about three days prior. Around eight o'clock, he began to call her back to back for an hour. She refused to answer.

After a week, she still wasn't prepared to talk to him. And now her relationship with Coco really made everything confusing for her. Sincere finally sent a message to her two-way.

Kisa, please call me. Its not about me; Mommy is in the hospital.

She immediately called him back. She was so nervous she could barely dial his number.

"Hello, hello.   Sincere, what's wrong with Mommy?"

"Kane, you have to get here; she is in a coma."

"What hospital?"

"We're at Harlem, room 335."

"I'll be there soon."

Kisa was unaware that Coco was standing behind her.

"Where are you going?"

"I have to leave now; Sincere's mother is in the hospital."

"What happened?"

"I don't know. I will call you when I know more."

Kisa all speed limits all the way from Westchester County to Manhattan.

When Kisa entered the room she was thrown into a state of shock. Lena had a bandage on her head, multiple bruises on her face, tubes in her nose, and a cast on her arm. Kisa had never seen anyone like this. Not even her friends that had been shot looked like this.

Sincere stood up and reached for Kisa's hand. She put her hand in his and hugged him. She could tell he'd been crying. Seeing him like this filled her with overwhelming guilt.

"Baby, I am so sorry. What happened?"

"I'm not sure. We stopped by Mommy's and the police were everywhere. Then I saw the paramedics putting her into the ambulance."

Kisa looked around the room at everybody and they all seemed so nervous. Eisani, Tyeis, and TaTa looked at her nervously as if they wanted to say something.

Butta stood on the opposite side of the bed from Sincere and Kisa. He stood there just rubbing Lena's hand. He would not even look up at Kisa.

Then Kisa finally noticed that there was something terribly wrong with the picture.

"Sincere, where is Kai?"

He tried to look her in the eye but couldn't bring himself to do it.

"Kisa, baby, I need you to listen."

Eisani came and stood next to her cousin.

"No Sin, where is my baby? That's a simple question."

He could not get it out quick enough for Kisa, so she turned to Eisani. "E, why isn't he answering me, E where is my baby? Somebody say something."

Sincere, finally able to speak, placed both hands on her shoulder. "Baby, she wasn't there. They took her."

"Who took her? The police?"

Sincere began shaking his head. "No Kisa, she was kidnapped."

"Nooo!" Kisa screamed, doubling over as if she was sick to her stomach. She began crying and throwing up.

Once she stopped throwing up, she started yelling again. "Sincere, find my baby! I need her. Who did this?" Eisani tried to comfort her. She began swinging her arms like a small child throwing a tantrum. She just continuously screamed as they tried to control her. "No, no, Lord, please, no."

Terry, who'd been standing watch by the door, put Kisa in a bear hug as a nurse came in and gave her a shot filled with a sedative. They laid Kisa out in a chair and let her sleep. There wasn't a dry eye in the room. Everyone was hurting for her.

The sedative had put Kisa out for hours. She had had nightmare after nightmare. She dreamed about Cuban Joe, with his face blown off, holding Kai. She had a dream about Shea being on the streets strung out on meth.

In her last dream, she dreamed that she was at the house in Jersey, playing on the carpet with Kai. The dream was so vivid that when she woke up, she thought she was really holding Kai in her arms. Then she looked over at Lena in the bed and remembered everything that had happened earlier.

She began to sob loudly. Sincere rushed in the room and hugged her. "Baby, I didn't think you was ever gonna wake up."

Kisa rested in his arms a few seconds before she spoke. "Sincere, does that crazy Milani bitch have my baby?"

"No, ma, Mannie and Terry already paid her a visit. I know for a fact it wasn't her."

"How can you be so sure? Oh, you must have been with her when it happened."

"Come on, Kisa, this ain't the time for that. But if you want to take it there, where the fuck you been for the last week and a half? I found out some very interesting info about your boy Coco, and Milani. Yeah, he paid her to push up on me. Not to get off the way more important issue of finding Kai. But I know you been with that nigga. And had you not been somewhere laid up with that nigga, this wouldn't have happened!"

Kisa went from sad to extremely angry in seconds. "First of all, you don't know shit about where I been. And if he did pay Milani, you are a grown-ass man! *You* made the decision to trick money on that bitch and take her on trips and to fuck her. And don't even try to make me feel guilty about this shit! I know I'm no angel, but it was probably some of your renegade enemies that took my daughter. And what makes you think what they did to Mommy, they wouldn't do to me?"

"She's my daughter too! Just like you're still my wife, in case you forgot while you were laid up fucking that nigga."

"Sincere *please*. Don't act like you give a fuck about me now! The only thing you can do for me is get my daughter back. After this is over with I want a divorce. And I don't want shit from you."

The sound of Sincere's cell phone interrupted the argument.

A voice that sounded almost computerized began to speak. "Sincere."

"Who is this?" Sincere demanded.

"Who I am is not important! What is important is how much you'll pay to get this sweet baby girl back."

"Nigga, how much you asking? We just want our daughter back safe."

"Punk, get six mill up, and I will call you back in a couple of days!" CLICK.

Kisa was anxious. "Sincere what did they say?"

"They want six million."

"When?"

"They said they'll call back in a couple of days."

"Did you tell the police they took Kai?"

"No."

"Why not?"

"Why are you asking me that? Like I'm not the coke man. Now if we need to get the jakes involved we will."

"Was Mommy able to speak to anyone before she slipped into the coma?"

"I talked to her neighbor and she said she saw two men leaving the apartment. When she got to Mommy she said Mommy told her to tell me they took Kai. Then she passed out."

Kisa started sobbing again. "My poor baby, she must be so terrified." Sincere's heart became flooded with guilt. He had already put her through so much drama. And no matter what, she stood by him patiently waiting for him to get his shit together. At this point, it didn't matter where she had been, who she was with, or what she had done. He had already forgiven her. Like everything else they had been through, he was determined to get through this too. And it still had not hit him that his daughter had been kidnapped. He bent down and hugged Kisa.

"Ma I didn't mean any of that shit I was saying. Kisa, can you please forgive me? Please forgive me for everything. "I can't lose you. After last week, I was so scared that I... I couldn't take it. It drove me crazy not having you around. I promise, baby, this time. Never again, I will never cheat again."

"Sin, you always say the same thing when you are caught out there. What makes this time different?"

Sincere took a deep breath. "Baby, we'll have to take everything one day at a time, but I swear to God, I will never do you wrong again. I'm going to get our daughter back and then we are going to live like a real family. Especially you and me. We're going to act like a real married couple. We're going to *be* a real married couple and do as married people do. If it's not business, we're not going to be in the streets. We're going to be in the house raising our daughter."

"Sincere, I'll come home, but I swear on everything I love, if you hurt me again, I'm out!"

"Baby, I promise you, it will be different. I love you, Kisa."

"I love you too. Now go find out where my daughter is so we can get her back."

Five days had gone by and still, no word from the kidnappers. Lena was still in a coma. Sincere scoured the streets looking for information, and Kisa spent most of her time at Lena's bedside. She had only changed twice in five days. Eisani and Tyeis had to force her to at least come to their homes and eat.

One night she went to Tyeis's apartment to eat. She had a funny feeling when she got to the door. Once inside she knew why. There was Bless and Coco sitting on the couch. Coco jumped up as soon as he saw her. "Kisa, are you okay? Ty told me what happened. Why didn't you call me and let me know what was going on?"

"Coco I'm okay now. Well, I'm okay for my circumstances. But I do need to speak to you in private. Can you come in the bedroom?"

Kisa wasted no time getting to the point. As soon as he closed the door she turned around and confronted him. "Look, I know about you and that Milani bitch. And I am not blaming just you. Like I told Sin, he is a grown-ass man, and he could have said no. I am more upset at you because I feel betrayed. The entire time you laid there holding me, you knew what was going on. And I'm not holding any grudges. I forgave him, so I forgive you. Right Sincere and I are working everything out. So there will be no more me-and-you. Please don't pursue me anymore; I'm going through enough as it is, and I don't need any extra shit. I'd like for us to end on a good note this time, so thank you for everything." She'd said all that in one breath, kissed him on his cheek, gave him a hug, and exited the room.

Coco stood with a dumbfounded look on his face. He had been so close. But he knew he had to really leave it alone now. He had to let her go. He had no choice; her heart belonged to Sincere.

Meanwhile, in a housing project in Washington D.C., Kai sat in a high chair. She wasn't terrified, unlike Kisa had imagined. She had no reason to be. She was just as giggly and comfortable as if she was with her own mother. That's because she was with the next best thing-her Aunt Shea.

Shea had no intentions of hurting Kai. Kai was one of the few people she did love. She just needed the money and knew Kisa would give her own life for that baby. So getting money was nothing. She had even considered taking Kai with her after the money drop and passing her off as her own daughter. But that was way to dangerous, even for Shea.

She knew that Kisa would stop at nothing to get Kai back. The whole scheme was dangerous enough. It was worse than setting Kisa up to be robbed last year.

But this time it was different. She had some renegade niggas out of D.C. who were about their paper. They wouldn't run their mouths like that coke-head, Cuban Joe.

After this lick, Shea told herself; *I can move out to Cali and live happily ever after.* She picked Cali, 'cause she was thinking of the place she would least likely run into Kisa. Kisa was an east coast chick to her heart, and she refused to even think about moving to the west side.

Shea had no clue that the niggas, who, had done the job, Ron and Bobby Mack had beat Lena up. They only knew not to hurt the baby. They had no plans on hurting Lena, but she'd put up a terrible fight for her grandbaby.

And Ron, he was a schizo. So when Lena hit him he hit her back and refused to stop. Bobby had to pull him away so they could leave. Now, as they sat across the table from Shea, Ron was getting real impatient with her. Shea couldn't make up her mind about when she wanted to exchange Kai for the money.

"Yo, come on, Shea. When we gonna drop this little whining bitch off and get that paper?"

"Look, let's give it a couple more days; we have to plan this drop carefully. We can only give them time to bring the money to the spot. We cannot give them time to plan anything extra, cause if we give them too much notice; it will get fucked up. Sincere is very smart. And stop disrespecting my niece!"

"I'll call you a *bitch, BITCH!* And fuck all this waiting shit. You trying to play us like we not straight murderers. Stupid hoe, we ain't none of them pussy-ass New York niggas you used to. We about our paper! So get your shit together, while me and Bobby plan this shit, and we going tonight. And hurry the fuck up 'for I fuck you and this lil' whining bitch up like I did her grandmother!"

"What?" Shea yelled. "Bobby, what the fuck is he talking about? What happened? I know y'all didn't do nothing to Sincere's mother."

Bobby knew that Ron wasn't playing with her. He grabbed Kai out of the highchair and pushed Shea into the bedroom.

"Shea, please just get your shit together, whatever you're taking. You know that nigga is psycho."

"BM, you have to tell me what happened."

"Look, she got in the way and Ron roughed her up."

"Come on, y'all shouldn't have done that. Now that nigga Sin gonna be beasting. He gonna want niggas to bleed for that. I mean, taking Kai was one thing; He already seeing red behind that shit. And he probably would have let that go as long as she was returned safe. Now he really gonna want war. Fuck me! I can't believe this shit."

"Look, we got you. Just pack while I calm this nigga down so we can work the details out. Stop worrying I'll take care of everything," Bobby told her as he walked out.

Back in Harlem, Kisa sat next to Lena's bed. Kisa looked like she was barely alive. Her face was pale, her hair in a ponytail. And she had not changed clothes in three days. She had not received her daily call from Sincere yet. They had agreed that he would only call once a day to check-in and let her know if he had found out anything new. Kisa hated this method, but if he called too much, it would only upset her if he didn't have anything new to tell her.

Kisa went to the restroom to freshen up and change her under clothes. While in the restroom, she heard Lena groaning. She rushed to her side. "Lena are you awake? Oh my God. Let me get the Doctor."

Lena reached and grabbed Kisa's arm tightly before she could get away. "Wait," she groaned, "Give me some water." Kisa held the straw up to Lena's mouth until she finished. When Lena finished, she motioned for Kisa to come closer. She cleared her throat and began to speak.

"From the way you look I can tell they still got my grandbaby. I'm sorry, but I fought as hard as I could."

"No, Lena, it's not your fault. You don't have to apologize."

"Yes I do baby, I have to apologize for all these years I turned my head. I watched Sincere and Butta do wrong. Then Sincere dragged you down with him when you were trying to do right. I promised myself he would never hustle like his father, who is dead, and my father, who sits in prison. I knew all these things yet I turned my head and took the money. Now I have to stop turning my head and speak up; it is too far out of control. I should have spoke up when you got robbed while you were pregnant with Kai. Now they have gone and taken your child. I pray to God that baby is okay. I already know she is though. Once you get her back, the both of you have to leave this game alone. Do you understand?"

"Mommy, I understand completely, but I've tried to make Sin stop. I've talked to him time after time, but he swears he can't get out until the time is right." Kisa began to cry.

"Baby, I know these are trying times for you," said Lena. "And it seems like there is no way out. You have to keep your faith; you have to keep yourself together, and your family. Now I want you to go down to Brooklyn and see my father. He'll help you get through to Sincere; he'll let you know what you have to do. This is the only way to get all the evil out your life once and for all. Until you make everything right, nothing good will come to you two."

Kisa took down the information Lena gave her so that she could go to Brooklyn. Kisa kissed Lena and said her goodbyes. She notified the doctor that Lena was awake and went on her mission, a mission to keep her family together and end all the *drama*.

Track 11: Somebody's Got to Die!

Kisa arrived at the Metropolitan Detention Center in Brooklyn the next morning. She had been granted a special visit, after speaking with the prison counselor. Kisa exaggerated Lena's condition, telling the counselor, "Mr. Tucci's daughter may not make it through the night."

Kisa had called Sincere, the night before to tell him that Lena had awakened. She was sure that he and Butta had spent the night at the hospital since Sincere didn't come home.

Once Kisa passed through security check, she waited patiently for Sincere's Grandfather to enter the visitation room.

It was clear that he was Sincere's grandfather. Although he was one hundred percent Italian, he had the same face and striking features as his daughter and grandson. He looked good for a seventy-years-old man, especially one in prison. Kisa stood up to greet him as the guard brought him in.

"Hi Mr. Tucci I am Sincere's wife Kisa Montega."

He greeted her with warmth. "Yes, sweetheart, I know who you are, and you're more beautiful than the pictures Sincere sent of the wedding."

"Thank you, Mr. Tucci."

He smiled and embraced her as if Kisa was his own daughter, "You're family; please call me Poppa Tucci."

Kisa sat down directly across from him.

He could look in her eyes and tell that she was very tired and stressed out. "Kisa, when they told me I had an emergency visitor, and it was you, I thought Sincere would be here also. Since he's not I have to ask, is he okay?"

"Yes, he's fine. As a matter of fact, he doesn't know I'm here."

"Well, what's wrong? It can't be that beautiful great-granddaughter of mine. Now that's who you should have brought."

At that instant Kisa broke down into tearful sobs.

Poppa Tucci did not know what to do. "Kisa, sweetie, are you okay? What's wrong? What did I say?"

Kisa gathered herself. "I'm sorry I broke down like that. Sometimes they come in waves. Some days I don't even break down until someone mentions Kai's name. Mr.... I mean, Poppa Tucci, Kai has been kidnapped, and I just feel like I'm running out of options."

Poppa Tucci sat intensely as she told him the entire story, from she and Sincere's break up to when Lena woke up the day before. When Kisa finished the story he was overwhelmed and disappointed.

"Why didn't Sincere come and tell me this? Why didn't anyone contact me before now? I can't believe no one thought to tell me about my daughter being in a coma."

"I thought you knew that much. I knew Sincere wasn't involving too many people until he found out exactly what we were up against. I swear to you, that I thought he would have at least called you. I came because Lena told me you're the only one who could help me get through to him. She said you're the only one who could get Sin out of this game. I've tried time and time again, and every time, he just tells me *soon*. Can you please help me get through to Sin?"

"That's the least of your worries. From this point on, you can consider Sincere Montega out of the

Business. And are you certain you've told me everything, Kisa?"

"Yes, I'm Positive. I'd never hold back, not with Kai's life on the line."

"You said the kidnappers want six million dollars?"

"Yes."

"Do you have it all to put up? Can you afford to put it up by yourselves and be okay if you don't get it back? Because Sincere knows I can give it to you."

"Thank you, Poppa Tucci, but we have more than enough."

At that moment, a young, good-looking black guard entered the room. He looked at Kisa who was holding hands with Tucci across the table, and gave her a look that said, *I know you're not messing with that old white man.*

Tucci noticed the look on his face. "Marcus, you can stop wondering. This is my grandson's wife."

"Oh no Mr. Tucci, sorry I just came to tell you that your time was up. Actually it's been up for ten minutes I was just procrastinating about coming in. You know I looks out."

"Thanks Marcus. Just let me say good bye and I will be ready to go back."

"That's fine. I'll be right outside."

He turned his attention back to Kisa. "Sweetie, I have to go now. Give me a hug, and stop beating yourself up so much. I'm going to put in some phone calls to help assist you and Sincere if you need it."

"Thank you so much, Poppa Tucci."

As he walked out the door, he told Kisa, "Don't hesitate to call or come see me again for anything."

As Kisa drove uptown she felt better already. She had decided to go to the apartment to get some rest before going to check in on Lena.

When she walked through the door it looked like a slumber party. Butta was sleeping on the couch, Terry and Shawn were sleeping on the floor, and Mannie was on the love seat.

She went into the bedroom; Sincere was lying diagonal across the bed. He was in a deep sleep. She sat next to him and gently woke him up. "Sincere, Sincere, wake up, baby."

He raised up groggily. "Hey, Kane, baby where've you been all day? I was trying to call you."

"I was out of the area so I couldn't get any reception. Why didn't you hit me on the two-way radio?"

"I tried, but something is wrong with my speaker I meant to go by Nextel and exchange it. Where were you at out of the area?"

"I had to take care of some business down in Brooklyn. Why are y'all dressed in black like y'all went to war?"

Sincere sat up and faced Kisa. His face became so intense. He saw the way her facial expression changed, like she was preparing for the worse.

"Baby, don't tense up on me; hear me out first. As far as I know, Kai is alright. I talked to the Kidnappers around 4 a.m."

"Sincere, why didn't you call me then? What did they say?"

"We're going to do the drop sometime around eleven tonight, and they're going to call us right before then. The only catch is they want you to come alone. I told them never. So Butta is going with you. I told them no money until you know Kai is okay. If they're smart, they'll be watching to make sure it's just the two of you. We're trying to get around that, but we're putting a tracking device in the bag with the money. And we may have one up on them anyway."

"How?"

Sincere hesitated. "Sincere what is it? Spit it out, I can handle anything right now. Please, just tell me?"

"Okay, okay, I been keeping tabs on Shea."

"What?"

"I couldn't help but feel that as long as she lives she will be a threat to us. So I've been paying her so-called friend Bunny, to keep me informed."

"So what are you getting at?"

"My instincts were right. Shea is back in the area with two niggas out of D.C. and some girl. Now I don't know who the bitch is, but the two niggas supposed to be some wild stickup kids, and one of 'em is a wild murderer. I had them all tracked down to the Marriott in Teaneck. Shea was seen carrying a toddler, but my man couldn't tell if it was Kai. He said the baby was wearing a pink hoodie with *DKNY baby* on the back."

"Sincere, I bought that jogging suit for Kai. That had to be her."

"Baby, I already figured it was her. I put it all together. The two niggas are the ones who beat up Mommy and took Kai. I got someone tracking them. I wanted to run up on them but I can't put Kai in that type of danger. Kisa, I know its her! *I swear to God!*"

Sincere just blew up and started yelling more.

"Fuck that, Kisa! I had a feeling it was her! This whole thing had her name written all over it! That bitch took my baby and left my mother for dead! I'm going to snap her neck! Fucking bitch. I hate her! Why didn't you just let us kill her?"

Sincere slammed his fist into the mirror, shattering the glass. He fell to his knees, crying. For the first time since the kidnapping he had broken down.

Butta, Terry, Shawn, and Mannie came running into the room. They were unaware that Kisa had came in.

"What's going on?" Butta asked.

Kisa motioned for them to go back. It took a couple of seconds for them to move. They had never seen Sincere so distraught. They slowly backed away from the door and Butta closed it.

Kisa knelt down beside him and wrapped him in her arms.

He was breathing heavy and still crying, "Why'd she ever have to be a part of our lives? I know she's your sister, but what kind of evil lives in her? How could she plot on her own niece?"

Kisa knew it was her turn to be the stronger one. "Come on, Sin, baby, get up. Sweetie, I need you to stand up."

Kisa pulled the covers back and helped Sincere lie down. She laid down beside him.

"Baby, let's rest a while. Your body is drained. You need more sleep."

"Kisa how did you stay with a fucked up nigga like me so long?"

"I ask myself that all the time, but I've never loved anyone like I love you and Kai. You're my family, and that's all that matters. And I've never met a perfect family."

Sincere fell asleep in Kisa's arms. She slept with him for a while. She could not get into the rhythm of sleeping, so she got up after while and showered. She didn't realize it was already three o'clock, *Hopefully I will I have Kai back in about eight hours.*

From the beginning it had ran through her mind that it might have been Shea. But she'd put that to the back of her mind, thinking, *Shea would never stoop that low.*

Kisa knew that Shea had to die. Kisa had been talking to the Lord a minimum of five times a day, saying the Rosary prayer, and she had even to went to confession. As she stood looking at herself in the shattered mirror, she realized that it was also a reflection of her own shattered life. She began to cry.

She dropped to her knees in prayer.

"Heavenly Father, thank you for life and all that's in it. Lord, thank you for the good and the bad, for the bad makes us stronger. Lord please forgive us for our sins and have mercy on our souls. And please don't let the sins of the mother and father be the sins of the child. Lord you blessed me with Kai and I still thank you. Please don't let evil take her away. I never really understood love until I met her. Please let her live her life, even if it means I have to lose my own. Lord I would love to be here to raise her and to guide her, but I know your will is your will. Please, Lord, whatever situation she's in, let your angels band a fence around her protecting her, from all hurt, harm, and danger. Lord, please continue to watch over us and protect us. These and all other blessings we ask in your holy and righteous name. In the name of the Father, the Son, and the Holy Spirit, Amen."

Sincere was still sleeping. Kisa was too jittery to sleep. She put on a black Sean John jogging suit and a pair of field Timberlands. She knew she had to thug-it for this mission. She could not sit still. So she went in the kitchen to cook dinner. Butta was sitting at the table drinking a cup of coffee spiked with Hennesy.

"What up, ma?"

"Nothing, brotha, what's the deal with you?"

"I can't call it. How's Sin holding up?"

"I don't know; he's still sleeping. I think he just needed to let it all out. He always lets everything build up until he explodes."

"How are you holding up?"

"I'm okay. I'll be better once I have my daughter back."

"I feel you. So I know he told you it's Shea."

"And you know it."

Butta took a big gulp of his coffee, not knowing how to make the next comment. "Kisa, you know she got to die this time."

"Trust me, I know!" Kisa replied.

He could see that she was carrying the weight of the world on her shoulders.

He could feel her grief as he thought, *How does one face the fact of having to kill their sibling or knowing that their sibling is going to be killed.*

Kisa got up and shook it off. "Butta do you want something to eat?"

"Yeah, what you cooking?"

"Some chicken, rice, and plantains."

"Go ask everybody else do they want some."

Kisa finished cooking. After she'd served everyone she took a plate to Sincere. He was still sleeping,

"Sincere, baby, wake up."

"Baby, what time is it?"

"Its fifteen after six."

"Damn, bay, why you let me sleep so long?"

"Cause you needed it. Here, eat this. I know you ain't ate."

"Come sit with me while I eat. How are you feeling, Kane?"

"I'm feeling aight for what I'm going through. Do you feel better now that you have let everything out?"

"I feel much better. I even feel lighter. I didn't mean to go 7:30 on you like that earlier."

Kisa interrupted him before he could finish. "No, baby, don't be sorry. I completely understand."

He didn't realize he was staring at her face not saying anything.

"Sincere, why are you looking at me like that?"

"Huh?" he asked, snapping out of his trance. "Oh, nothing really. Just thinking. After all this is over, we're going away for a while. Just go away and relax; put all this bullshit behind us. And no more of this street shit. I know the streets gave us everything. But we're not enjoying it, so we're not happy."

"Sin, are you serious? Are you getting out of the game?" she asked with a very hopeful expression.

"I was thinking about it."

Kisa's expression changed rapidly, and he noticed it. "No, baby, what I mean is I already had been thinking about it. I also know why you went to Brooklyn today."

"How did you know?"

"Oh, you know Mommy had a long conversation with me last night, and she let it slip out. Then Poppa Tucci called me and said no more. He even told Corletti not to supply me with any more coke. He asked me did we have enough to live off of. He told me if we didn't, he would give it to us. I told him we weren't wanting for anything. And between my stores and your salons we should be covered for years. Plus I set Corletti up with Butta, and for a year I'll get a percentage off of every brick he sells."

Kisa was so excited. Then her smile turned to a frown.

"Kisa, what's wrong? What did I say?"

"You didn't say anything; I shouldn't be smiling yet. I can't smile until we get our baby girl back."

"Baby, don't worry. We are going to get our baby back in a few hours."

He hugged her and kissed her on the forehead. They stayed embraced for a while until Sincere's cell phone rang.

"Damn! Where is my phone?"

"It sounds like it's in your coat pocket on the chair."

He finally found the ringing phone. "Hello? When? Are you sure?"

Kisa waited anxiously for him to finish the conversation.

"BK, you have to stay with them. I'm going to get Kane and these niggas ready to go. I'll be in the car riding around waiting for your call. One."

Kisa didn't even wait for him to remove the phone from his ear. "Baby, what did BK say?"

"He said Shea and them niggas just left the hotel and she definitely had Kai with her."

"What?" Kisa yelled. "Why didn't you tell him to run up on them and knock that bitch out and get my baby back?"

"No, Kisa. We have to play it safe. I want you and Kai out of the way completely before anything goes down."

"Sincere, I need to see Shea."

Sincere started to get dressed quietly, then he pulled two large duffel bags from the closet. He opened them; each bag was filled to the top with all one hundred dollar bills.

"Sincere, do you hear me?"

"Yeah, I hear you. Baby, you can't save her this time she's done too much."

"I'm not trying to save her. She's endangered my child. I just have to see her."

Sincere could see a strange look in her. "Kisa baby, I can't let you kill her; you're not built for this one. I never meant for that shit to go down like that with Cuban. After that shit, you had nightmares for weeks. So, no, ma. I need you, and Kai needs you."

Sincere picked up the bags and kissed Kisa.

"Ma, stop crying. Get your self together. I'm going to let these niggas know what's up. Be ready to go down stairs in a half hour."

Kisa cried her last tear, washed her face and grabbed her glock .380. She placed it in the small of her back and proceeded to the living room. "I'm ready."

Sincere turned and looked at her. "Are you sure?"

"I'm Sure."

"Let's roll. I'm going to ride with you and Butta until I get the call."

They all rode around the city for hours, waiting for the call, jumping anytime anyone's phone rang. A couple of times it was Eisani and Tyeise calling to see if they had heard anything.

Sincere repeatedly gave Kisa the instructions. "Look, Kisa, I want you to give the niggas the money and get Kai back so we can secure y'all and handle these niggas. Better yet, if BK can tell us exactly how they're set up, while you're doing the money drop, we'll get Kai. When everything is straight, I'll hit you on the radio and give you the signal. Don't worry about the money. Regardless, we can track them down."

Kisa just nodded her head in agreement. They continued to ride around at 10:50p.m. Sincere received the call. He talked for a minute and hung up. As soon as he finished Kisa was on him.

"Who was that?"

"The kidnappers. They want you to come to an abandoned building off of Boston Road in the Bronx."

Sincere's phone rang again. He looked down at the caller ID. "This is BK right here. Kane, hit Mannie on his radio and tell him to pull over."

Sincere answered his phone. "What's good?"

He listened closely to every word BK spoke.

"Aight, stay there; I'm coming with Mannie, Shawn, and Big Terry. Aight, my nigga, it's on. One."

Sincere briefed Kisa and Butta on the situation. "BK said the two niggas just left the room, but Shea and that bitch is there with Kai. I'm going over there to try to get Kai out now. I'll hit y'all on Kisa's radio to give you the signal that I already have Kai. If I ask you, is the *drop over?* That means I have Kai and get out. Don't worry about the money just break out."

He turned to Kisa. "Ma, this is it. We're going to get her back."

"I know, baby, so no fuck-ups. I want her sleeping in the bed with me tonight."

"And she will be; I promise you that. Now give me a hug."

They held each other for a few seconds, but it felt like an eternity.

Kisa looked him in the eyes and said, "No matter what happened or what happens, I need you to know that I never stopped loving you."

"I know ma, and I never stopped loving you." Sincere and Butta exchanged silent pounds, as Sincere exited the truck and got into Mannie's truck.

Butta drove to the abandoned building and parked. He looked over at Kisa. "You ready, Kane?"

Kisa stared at a lonely light that shined through a foggy window. "I'm as ready as I'm ever gonna be."

They exited the truck, both carrying one of the duffel bags. As they walked towards the partly dilapidated building, Kisa's heart began to race.

They stepped inside a steel door that was coated with graffiti. At first they saw no one.

Then Ron and Bobby stepped from behind a raggedy staircase, wearing hockey masks. Ron yelled out to them as he aimed a gun at them. "Stay right there and drop the paper."

Kisa yelled back, "We're not dropping nothing until I know my daughter is okay?"

Bobby stepped forward, holding a camcorder. He pointed at Kisa. "Give the bag to your partner and come here."

She turned and gave the bag to Butta. Butta gave her a look that said, *don't go.* Kisa gave him the signal to let him know that she had her glock. She walked over to Bobby and he held up the camcorder so she could she the screen.

It was a recording of Kai, playing with building blocks, on what appeared to be a hotel bed. Kisa's eyes became filled with tears. "My baby is okay."

Bobby told her, "Look at the date and time. That was today, only a hour ago."

"Okay, but when am I going to get her back physically?"

"After we check the paper, we'll tell you where to go."

Kisa turned and walked to Butta. "You can give them the bags. She's okay."

Ron continued to hold the gun on Butta as he dropped the money at Bobby's feet. The light on Kisa's Nextel was blinking like someone was trying to radio her, but she never heard anything come through.

On the inside she was frantic, thinking, *What's Sin trying to tell me?*

Sincere was less than three minutes away from Kisa. He had already gotten Kai out of the hotel room. He was waiting for Shawn and Terry to finish tying Shea up.

Terry had kicked the room door open. Ron's girlfriend tried to pull a burner and blast on them. Terry shot her in the chest. Sincere was glad that Terry had used silencer and he was thankful that Kai was sleeping.

He scooped her up in a blanket and took her to the truck. Now he was trying, unsuccessfully, to get through to Kisa. Terry came out the room carrying Shea over his shoulder, followed by Shawn and BK.

Sincere rolled down the window. "Yo, Terry, you and Shawn ride with BK. Put that bitch in between y'all and make sure she don't try nothing slick."

By now Kisa was beginning to sweat as Bobby looked through the second bag. She was praying that he wouldn't find the tracking device.

Bobby looked over at Ron to let him know the paper was straight.

Bobby looked at Kisa. "Aight, Miss Lady wait here for fifteen minutes. Go out of here and make a right onto Boston Rd. There is a McDonald's. Behind that McDonald's sits a hotel. Your baby is in room 220."

Ron, still holding the gun on them said, "And Wait fifteen minutes. Do not attempt to follow us."

Then sarcastically he said to Kisa, "It was nice doing business with you ma'am."

Kisa wanted so bad to pull her piece out and blast on them, but she didn't know her daughter's predicament, and wouldn't dare risk it.

The door opened, and in walked Terry followed by Sincere, Shawn, and BK all with their gats raised.

You could hear Bobby gasp for his breath and see his eyes get big through the mask. Ron kept his gun aimed at Butta.

Terry told him as he held the gun next to Shea's head, "Don't move or this bitch is dead!"

Ron took his mask off. "You think I give a fuck about that bitch, I was gonna smoke her grimy ass anyway."

Kisa stood in the middle of all the grown men who were holding raised guns, each one contemplating a good game of gunplay.

She turned to Sincere. "Where is my baby? Is she okay?"

"She is fine; she's in the truck with Mannie. Go on and get in the truck so he can get y'all out of here."

Kisa turned and looked at Shea. Shea's eyes pleaded for forgiveness. She even tried to explain. "Kisa, you have to know I would never hurt her. I...I."

Kisa cut her off. "That's my child. I was going crazy not knowing if she was alive, if she was crying for me, or if she was even being fed. I can't save you this time. Besides, if I keep saving you, one day you're going to kill me or someone close to me. So if it's down to that, it's going to be you. And I never thought it would come to this."

If Shea had any chance of being saved by Kisa, she messed that up by saying, "Fuck you, Kisa. I hate you, 'cause you hate me. What kind of bitch is willing to let her own sister die and do nothing to stop it?"

"A real bitch." Kisa said as she turned to walk towards the door. Then she felt a hard bang on her shoulder. She never heard the shot. It burned so bad she fell to her knees. Then she felt the second wave of heat in her right thigh.

Sincere could not believe what had just happened. Ron had shot Kisa twice. All of a sudden bullets were flying, Terry pushed Shea out in front of him. Her body became riddled with bullets and covered in blood.

Sincere hit Ron in the forehead with one clean shot that sent him flying backwards.

When all the fire ceased, Bobby was on the ground full of holes, shaking like he was having a seizure. Terry started to shoot him again, but he knew he was dead. There was blood running down his nose and out his mouth.

Sincere ran to Kisa who was lying on the cold cement floor, blood gushing from her thigh and trickling down her shoulder. "Kisa, baby, hold on. We're going to get you to the hospital. Butta, help me get her to the truck."

Butta rushed to the other side of the room only to be sickened by the sight of Kisa's body. "Sin, you have to put pressure on her shoulder. I'll tie my du-rag around her leg to slow the bleeding. She is losing a lot of blood."

Everyone looked on in silence as Sincere and Butta prepared Kisa. They finally picked her unconscious body up off the floor.

BK asked Sincere, "Do you need any help?"

"Nah just help Shawn and Terry get rid of those bodies and call me when you finish."

As they approached the truck, Mannie put Kai down in the passenger seat, jumped out, and opened the back door.

"What in the hell happened in there? I thought Kisa was coming out."

With shakey voice Sincere answered, "One of them fuckers shot her before she could get out."

Sincere got in the truck first and placed Kisa's head in his lap.

Kai turned around and saw Kisa. She reached for her and called out, "Ma-Ma, Ma-Ma."

The tears ran down Sincere's face.

"Butta, put her on your lap and keep her turned around. Kisa, baby, you have to hold on; Kai needs you. Mannie drive faster."

Kisa was able to open her eyes a little but everything was so blurry. She could see Kai's head and her little ponytails. She began to whisper her name. "Kai, Kai."

Sincere heard her struggling to speak. "Kisa don't talk. Save your breath baby."

"Sincere, take care of my baby. If I don't make it, let her know how much I loved her."

"No, Keesy, baby, you have to fight, and you're going to make it. Do it for Kai. Remember, her first birthday party is next month."

Butta squeezed Kai tight with tears streaming down his face. Even Mannie had tears running down his face. Sincere began yelling for Mannie to drive faster.

"Calm down," Mannie responded. "We're right here; get ready to get her out."

He pulled into the emergency entrance of Bronx Lebanon hospital, blowing his horn like a maniac.

He jumped out the truck almost before it was in park, yelling, "I have a gunshot victim."

Three ER doctors, who were standing outside smoking cigarettes, got a stretcher. As they put her on the stretcher, she told Sincere, "Baby, it's starting to feel better."

He knew she was beginning to slip away. As they rolled her away the doctor yelled out.

"Prep the OR; I have a gunshot victim who's lost a lot of blood. She's fading fast let's get her back, people."

Sincere stood in the hallway, blood-soaked and crying. He turned to Mannie and asked him, "Would you pray with me?" Mannie gave Sincere his hand and they knelt down. Sincere said the prayer of the Rosary, then a personal one. "God, thank you so much for returning my little girl safely. Can you please save my wife? I love her so much. I promise I'll never take her for granted again I'll never cheat again. I'll work hard to make her happy, and I'll always take care of home first. God, if not for me, please do it for Kai. I love you and thank you for your many blessings. In the name of the Father, the Son, and the Holy Ghost, Amen."

Two and half-hours later, TaTa, Tyeis, Eisani, Butta, and Mannie were all there trying to be a comfort to Sincere and Kai.

Eisani was not much help. She was pretty inconsolable herself. Finally the doctor came in. His face was very red. By the expression on his face, everyone knew it was bad news. He took a deep breath before he spoke. "Mr. Montega, we put up a hard fight...So far, we are winning."

Everyone let out a sigh of relief.

"Mrs. Montega is in recovery right now. She is in stable but very serious condition. So she'll be under observation for 24 hours. She lost a tremendous amount of blood, but she is lucky that both bullets went clean through without hitting anything major."

Sincere stood up to shake the doctor's hand. "Thank you so much, Dr. Davidson. When can we see her?"

"She'll be in her room in about two hours. You can go in, but she'll probably not wake up until mid afternoon. And oh, no one asked about the baby?"

"What baby?" Everyone asked at the same time.

"She appears to be about seven and a half weeks pregnant. The baby is fine despite what she has been through."

They all finished thanking the doctor. Sincere went in a private corner and said a prayer, this time just he and Kai.

Kisa woke up the next day around three o'clock. She didn't remember everything right away. She felt the tubes in her nose. Her mouth was dry and pasty. Then all the events of the previous night came back to her. She looked around and the room was empty, but she could hear voices outside her door. "Sincere." She could barely hear her own voice, so she called out again. "Sincere." It was louder but not loud enough. "SINCERE!"

It hurt but she'd got her point across. Sincere came running in the room, with Kai in his arms, followed by Eisani, TaTa, Tyeis, and Butta. He was smiling so hard he could barely keep from laughing.

"Kane, baby, I'm so happy you're okay. Here is Kai. She has been asking for you all day."

"Put her up here next to me."

Kisa lifted her head enough to kiss Kai. "Hi mommy's baby. I missed you so much. I promise I will never let anything happen to you again."

Kai said one of the few words that she knew. "Ma-Ma."

Hearing that made Kisa so happy, she cried tears of joy. Sincere sat down next to his wife, so happy to have her back from the verge of death.

"Baby I thought I almost lost you for a minute."

"You did, but God said it wasn't my time. So I kept fighting, so I could stay and raise Kai."

"And the new baby? Why didn't you tell us?"

"Really I just found out myself a couple a days ago. I planned on telling you after all this was over."

"I can feel you on that. So maybe I can get a boy out of you this time."

Sincere bent down and gave Kisa a long kiss. "I love you ma."

"I love you too, Poppi."

Eisani interrupted the spousal moment. "Okay, can we get a minute with our cousin, *PLALEEZ?*"

"I know that's right," Tyeis chimed in.

Eisani bent down and hugged Kisa. "Now you know you're never going anywhere with out us again, right?"

"Yes, Mama," Kisa joked.

Tyeis told Kisa, "And we're moving back in with you."

"Oh stars." Kisa laughed.

Then Eisani became serious.

"For real, ma, we already talked to Sincere, and he told us the deal. But now I'm saying it to you: no more street shit!"

"I know, E. You don't have to worry about that anymore."

TaTa, who had been too emotional to speak, finally opened her mouth. "Hi Kane. I'm happy you are okay baby. I don't know what I would have done if you would have..." She couldn't even finish the sentence. She broke down and ran out of the room. Eisani ran after her.

"She'll be okay," Tyeis said. "This is her first time crying. Oh yeah, we told the jakes we were on our way to meet Sincere when some kids tried to stick us. And

when we ran they shot you.　So get your story
together. They *will* be back tomorrow to question you."

"Thank you, Ty.　I love you."

"I love you too." Tyeis bent down and kissed her
on the cheek.

Butta stepped up next and gave Kisa a hug and
kiss.

"Here ma.　Someone wants to talk to you," he
said, handing her his cell phone.

"Hello?" Kisa said.

"Hi, Kisa, baby."

"Hi, Lena!"

"How you feeling, baby?"

"I'm feeling okay, Mommy."

"Well, baby, you did it."

"Yeah, with your help."

"No, I just gave you direction and you took it.
Now you have your family back; keep them together.
Everything you just went through will make you
stronger. And I mean everything should be a lesson,
from the beginning of you and Sincere to now."

"Mommy, for all it's worth, I would go through it
all again."

"I know you would, baby, 'cause you just a little
ghetto girl chasing dreams of diamonds and pearls."

Grindin' For Keeps
A Harlem Story
By
Danielle Santiago

Special Bonus Preview:

Danielle and 2 of A Kind Publishing Thank you for choosing *Little Ghetto Girl*. As a token of our appreciation, please enjoy the first two chapters of Danielle's upcoming book.

Chapter One: Vegas Nights

"*Damn*, Nina, how much of that shit did you put in his drink?"

"Same amount as usual. Why?"

"'Cause his ass looks dead."

Nina glanced at the middle-aged white man lying across the bed. He was in a deep sleep from the micky she had slipped him less than thirty minutes ago. "Kennedy, ain't nothing wrong with that man. He look like that 'cause he drank everything the bar had to offer! Just hurry and finish wiping everything down; we can not afford to get sloppy now."

"I'm through wiping. You hurry up and crack that safe so we can get that shit and be out."

Nina tried and tried but so far had been unsuccessful at cracking the code to the hotel room safe.

And Kennedy was becoming impatient. "Look, Nina, fuck whatever is in that safe; we got his Rolex and four thousand cash. We need to go ship this shit and catch our flight!"

Calmly, while never taking eyes away from the safe, Nina responded to her baby cousin. "Ken, I've always told you patience is a virtue."

"Haven't you noticed, I'm not big on virtues?"

"Besides I know this old bastard got way more paper in this safe. You should have seen how much he was spending on chips... about ten Gs a table. His bar tab was a G and he paid everything in cash."

Nina continued to give her full attention to the safe. She looked like a high fashion runway model, as opposed to hustler and part-time scam artist. She stood about 5'10, and she was slim but curvy in the right places. Her 36 D cups sat up nicely, enhancing the knee-length red Valentino red tube-dress that she was wearing.

Her legs were especially beautiful; her calves were more defined by the Manolo Blahnik stilettos. Tonight was her turn to attract the rich white Vegas gamblers with her smooth chocolate skin and her shoulder-length jet-black hair.

Once in their rooms, Nina slipped them a micky just to rob them blind.

Kennedy was the mastermind behind the scheme. At twenty-two, she was a genius at crimes. If it were a major in college, she would be graduated summa cum laude.

She'd come up with this particular scheme after the ATF and DEA had raided Nina and herself. The only thing that saved them from going to state or federal prison was the fact that thirty minutes before the raid, they had been robbed. Nina's disgruntled children's father and brother had hit them for four Kilos and all of their firearms. After everything was over, Kennedy looked at the robbery as a blessing.

Kennedy looked on, aggravated, as Nina continued to try and crack the safe's code. Suddenly Nina exhaled. "There, I did it. Told you ma just be easy." As she pulled the safe's door open, she could not believe what she was seeing. She covered her mouth with a gloved hand, to keep from screaming.

Kennedy got off the barstool and walked towards her cousin to see what the excitement was about. "Nina, what is it?"

"Yo, it must be fifty G's in here! And, Ken, look at this black bag. It looks like diamonds, ma."

"Nigga, let me see! Damn, it's like thirty loose stones in here. This nigga must be a criminal himself. Come on, bag all this up. Lets be out."

Kennedy drove back to their hotel on the out skirts of Las Vegas. She was tired and weary; they had checked-in four days ago. That meant four days of not much sleep and no play, and Kennedy's five foot seven frame showed it.

The night before, she worked three different casino hotels, getting four different men for their loot. She had cleared forty-five thousand dollars in cash and jewelry.

Tonight her appearance was different. Last night she was a glamour girl. Instead of black Gucci mini-dress she'd donned the night before, she wore a white tee and cut up jean shorts. A crispy white pair of uptowns replaced the Jimmy Choo stilettos. Her long reddish-brown hair was pulled back into a neat ponytail. Her beautiful makeup job was gone, her lips covered only by a hint of MAC lip glass.

Kennedy had to take No-Doze to stay awake while driving. Nina had already fallen into a deep sleep. Kennedy thought about playing a prank on her to get her up. She decided to let her cousin sleep for the remaining thirty minutes of the ride. Kennedy thought to herself, *Nina did a wonderful job tonight. She was so adamant about getting that safe open. The cash alone put us over a hundred g's for one day, and ain't no telling how much those diamonds are worth.*

After what felt like an eternal thirty minutes, they arrived at the hotel.

"Yo, Nina, get up. We're here. Come on, its six-fifteen already."

Without opening her eyes, Nina responded groggily, "Just let me sleep twenty more minutes."

"No. Get up! We have to pack all this shit up, ship it, and get to the airport by nine-forty-five in case you forgot our plane leaves at ten-fifty."

She rose up from the reclined seat with an attitude and fresh drool on her face.

"Alright, alright. Damn! You get on my nerves. Everybody ain't like you; I can't stay up for forty eight hours with no sleep."

"Nina, I don't want to hear that shit, you can sleep as long as you want when we get home."

"Stop bugging, chic, I'm up."

Inside the room they got right to the job at hand. Kennedy lined souvenir vases with cash and jewelry. Nina carefully wrapped each one in tissue paper and plastic bubble before placing them in the box.

After they had finished, Kennedy stood up and scanned the room to make sure nothing was left behind. "Is that everything Nina?"

"Yeah, ma, that's everything."

"Alright then, we only have forty-five minutes to get ready. I'll go ahead and get in the shower; I already have my clothes out."

They finished dressing, packed the rented Suburban, and headed for UPS. Kennedy was glad to see the same black man who had been there each day, working the counter.

He openly flirted with her, even though he was old enough to be her grandfather. He had even given her a discount on shipping. He began to smile, revealing a gold crown at the sight of Kennedy in a pair of tight Chloe jeans, a black halter-top and spiked sandals. Her tanned red skin and her beautiful smile entranced him. With his husky voice he greeted her, "Hey, young lady, I see you came back to see me."

Showing her pearly whites she responded, "And how are you this morning sir?"

"I'm a lot better now that I've seen your pretty face. Now tell me, did you come back to take me up on my offer of marriage?" The greasy old man and his gold crown literally made Kennedy sick. But with everything in mind, she played right along with him and flirted back, licking her lips and smiling as she answered. "Not this time, baby, but I will let you know next week."

"Girl, you can have all my money."

Kennedy thought to herself, *I'd rather be broke.*

She was tired of playing, so she got to the point. "I have to catch a flight to Louisiana, and I need to overnight these to my sisters in New York. I need to insure both boxes for ten-thousand dollars apiece."

"Damn, girl, what you got in the boxes, gold? You wanted the same amount on all those other boxes."

"Only thing in those boxes is antique vases. Only reason I insure them for so much is because I know they won't get messed up or stolen. If anything happens to them someone will lose their job when United Parcel Services has to kick out ten g's or more."

"Well look here, baby girl, just pay for the insurance, I won't charge you for the shipping and handling."

"Okay, that's what's up."

She paid him and turned towards the door. As she walked away, his eyes were fixed on her ass. He thought to himself, *I'm going to have some of that sweet young thing.*

When Kennedy approached the truck she saw Nina bending down in the seat. As she looked closer, she saw three white lines on Nina's compact mirror, and a rolled up fifty-dollar bill up her nose, her nostrils vacuumed the powder trails clean. Kennedy yanked the door open, jumped in, and began barking on Nina.

"What the fuck are you doing?"

"Come on, Ken-Ken with that self-righteous shit."

Kennedy cut her off, "No, Nina! I don't want to hear that shit. One, how can you even ride around with that shit knowing what we are out here doing? Come on, B, how fucking stupid is jeopardizing everything we came out here for over some fucking blow? Damn, bitch, are you twenty-nine or nineteen?"

Nina sat in disbelief at how her baby cousin had just blown up at her. "Kennedy, it's not that serious. I always have to toot a little powder before I get on the plane. You know I get nervous about flying."

"That's no excuse. You can get a doctor to prescribe you something for that. How long you been back on that shit? I thought you was clean."

Tears welled up in Nina's eyes as she thought back to a time when crack and heroine ruled her every move. At the time, Kennedy was only eighteen, but she had helped Nina to overcome her addiction. Their entire family had completely given up on Nina. At twenty-two, she was strung out with two kids. After nearly killing herself and her youngest son, she checked into a twenty-eight-day clinic.

No one had expected it to work; she had been there and done that so many times before. While she was away, for that particular stretch of sobriety, Kennedy got tired of hearing all their aunts talking about Nina like she was some stranger in the street. They were the same aunts who had kept their hands open for a hand out when Nina's money was long.

Furthermore, she was just sick of seeing the older cousin that she admired so much, fading away. All of her life, she had looked up to Nina; she liked the way Nina got her own paper. While most girls were begging boys for sneaker, doobie, and nail money, Nina was getting her hustle on. And Kennedy always thought her cousin was the flyest chic in Harlem, and the prettiest dark-skin girl she had ever seen.

The heroin addict that Nina had turned into was someone whom Kennedy did not know. Her meticulously neat cousin had been wearing the same clothes for days on end. Her smooth chocolate skin had become blotchy and dry. Her long, thick hair had become simply long and stringy.

At the end of the twenty-eight days, Kennedy was there to pick her up. She moved into Nina's house, cooked good meals for her, and took care of her sons. A year later, she was back on her feet and clean.

She was even more beautiful and healthier than before the drugs. It had been four years since Nina had closed the book on that chapter of her life. She could not deny that Kennedy was one of the few people who loved her unconditionally, and who was only barking on her out of true love.

Nina snapped back into reality. "Ken-Ken, I swear I only toot every now and then. Only when I'm completely stressed or I'm about to fly. And I promise you I'm not fucking with that heroine."

"Look, Nina, I love you no matter what, but I never want to see you go through that shit again. I'm not eighteen anymore; I don't have the energy to go through that shit with you again. And what about your kids? Niko and Taylor are old enough to know now. And Madeline is only two. She needs you to be there for her."

"Kennedy, I promise I'll never go back to that again."

"Aight, ma, whatever you say. But check this, whatever you got left, you need to toss it. I be damned if I get knocked for some petty blow shit."

Chapter 2: Home to Harlem

The ride to the airport and the flight home had been silent. Nina could tell that Kennedy was still upset. After they had picked up their luggage, they caught the shuttle to the parking deck and picked up Kennedy's X-5.

Once on the highway, Nina could not take the silence anymore. "Kennedy, I said I was sorry, so can you kill the cold shoulder act already?"

"Nina, I'm past that already, I'm quiet because I'm exhausted."

"Well what are you going to do tonight?"

"First, I'm going home and I'm going to sleep, and sleep, and sleep."

"When are you going to Aunt Karen's house to pick up the boxes?"

"Nina, I thought you were going to pick up everything."

"I can't. Once I pick up the truck, I have to drive all the way to Central Islip and pick up the kids from my stepmother's."

Kennedy was too tired to negotiate, so she gave in. "Well, I'll just wait until tomorrow so that the packages we sent this morning will be there too. Besides, I already have plans for tonight." Kennedy said with a sneaky smile on her face. Nina was curious about that smile. Everyone knew that Kennedy had not had a steady companion since she'd given birth to her son, Jordan, a year ago. "Ken-Ken who do you have plans with?" Nina asked still studying the expression on Kennedy's face.

"It ain't nothing special Hassan is coming over to hang with me."

"Hassan.   Who?   The rapper from Lincoln Projects?"

"Yes, Nina, the same Hassan."

"I didn't know you still fucked with him. Don't he still go with that same girl he been with forever?"

Kennedy looked at Nina from the corner of her eye. "Yeah, why? You gonna call her or something?"

Nina rolled her eyes. "No, bitch, don't play yourself. I'm just saying, you got mad niggas chasing you from everywhere, with crazy paper, trying to wife you. And you still fucking with this rapping nigga who got a bitch at home? Come on, what part of the game is that ma?"

Kennedy felt her face turning red. She kept her eyes on the road. "Are you through?"

"What?"

"Are you through expressing your opinion on my life."

"What are you talking about, Kennedy?"

"Look, ma, I like the way my relationship is with Hassan. The rules are clear and defined I know he got a girl. We don't lie to each other about the obvious. You heard what Hova said; *Our time together is our time together.* And as far as all these niggas out here chasing me, they don't want to do nothing but play with my mind. I've been through all the games before, and I ain't for it now. Plus I'm not trying to have no frivolous niggas around my son. I've been through too much. What you think I should do? Be like you and Cream? Well that's not the type of nigga I want in my cipher."

Nina folded her arms across her chest and began moving her neck as she started speaking.

"And what the fuck is that suppose to mean, Kennedy?"

"Oh *please*, don't play coy with me, ma. So what, you got a nigga at home! Are you happy with him? Tell me are you? How can you be happy with a man who punches you in the face whenever you say something he doesn't like? Or better yet, a nigga you caught fucking your best friend!"

An annoyed Nina finally interrupted Kennedy before she could go any further. "Please stop with all that bullshit you kicking! You making it sound worse than what it is. And so what he fucked that bitch? You see who he's with. And don't act like he just be hitting me for no reason because I do provoke him most of the time."

Kennedy nearly crashed from laughing so hard at Nina's last comment. Nina was frozen holding onto the dashboard. "Bitch, what is wrong with you?"

Kennedy, still laughing, replied, "I don't want you to say anything else to me just for saying that bullshit!"

"What Bullshit?" Nina asked, looking bewildered.

"That stupid shit you just said about you be provoking him. Ma, you really sound like you suffering from battered women's syndrome. That's exactly why I don't want you to call me no more when he choking your simple ass out."

"Oh, so you wouldn't help me if you saw that nigga beating me?"

"Fam, come on, don't even play me like that. Every time I jump in a fight between you two, you go right back to him. And let's not forget that night in NV when he was fucking your face up. And I hit him over the head with that Hypnotiq bottle. You had the nerve to buck up to me, screaming on me and shit, in front of all those people. I should have duffed your ass. So hell yeah, the answer is no."

"Damn, Ken, I didn't know the shit was that serious."

"Yeah, it's that serious, 'cause I can't understand how a bitch of your caliber be fucking with these bum-ass niggas. And no I'm not talking 'bout their financial status; I'm talking about their mental capacity."

Nina didn't want to discuss it anymore, so she just let it go with no response. Kennedy hated the way the day was going. They had never argued that much. But she really hated it when people tried to analyze her life, especially when they didn't have their own in check.

As Kennedy pulled into the garage, Nina began going off out of nowhere. "Damn Cream's ass! Nobody told him to come get my truck and leave this fucked up shit here." Nina pulled out her cell phone and made a call, with no luck.

Kennedy asked her, "What's wrong with the Lex? Don't you have keys to it?"

"Yeah, I got keys to it, but don't you see all those key scratches all over it?"

"Oh shit, yo, I didn't even peep that."

Nina hopped out of the truck and began tossing her bags into the back of the Lexus. Still heated, she walked over to Kennedy's side of the truck. "I know one of his bitches done keyed his car. I hate him so much. Anyway, what time do you want to hook up tomorrow?"

"Early! The rest of the boxes are supposed to be there by nine. We have to do everything early Nina, 'cause I'm going down south to get Jordan."

"You driving all the way to NC by yourself?"

"Nah, Kneaka is going to ride with me. Yesterday was the last day of summer school at Fordam."

"I might ride with you too; I need to go see my mother."

"Well, let me know.   I have to go I'm about to pass out. Holla back."

"One."

Kennedy drove down the hill to her apartment, she did not even bother to go to the garage to park. She was too tired to walk or catch a cab. She parked on the street down the block from her building.

Kennedy walked into her apartment and dropped everything by the door, including the mail she had picked up from the mailbox, not even bothering to look at it. She fell onto her bed, kicked off her shoes and with in seconds was in a deep sleep.

As Nina pulled up to her building, she saw her Benz truck parked on the opposite side of the street. Cream and about twenty other guys were standing by the truck playing C-Lo.

When Cream spotted Nina, he walked across the street, smiling from ear to ear. "Hey, Nee, baby, when did you get back? Give me a hug, ma." He grabbed her with his 6'5, well-built body and hugged her tight.

She squirmed until she broke free of his firm grasp. "Cream get the hell away from me before I smack your trifling ass. And take this keyed up shit so I can go get my kids."

"Ma, what the fuck is wrong with you? Why you breaking? Damn, ain't you happy to see your man?"

"I might be happy to see your ass if, when I came home, drama didn't hit me dead in the face."

"What are you talking about, Nina?"

"What am I talking about? Don't play stupid; you know what I'm talking about. That bitch keying your car up like this."

"No, I don't know what you're talking about, 'cause some little punks did that shit."

Nina was becoming furious. She hated when someone tried to play on her intelligence.

"Look, Cream, stop while you are ahead. If your lazy ass ever bothered to check the voicemail, you would know she left me a long message concerning your relationship with her. Oh, you don't believe me? Her name is Tasha Eaton and she said she is pregnant by you. And before she became pregnant, you was all in love with her, spending money, taking her on trips with you and your boys. And the two of you even have a little love nest over in Lenox Terrace. But as soon as she said she was pregnant by you, that is the first time you ever mentioned Maddy or me to her. And you told her she better get an abortion."

Nina had given him the entire synopsis from the top of her lungs, so everyone in the street was staring. It was already a hot July day, and Nina's confrontation really made Cream sweat even more.

His crisp white tee and baggy jean shorts were soaked in perspiration. He looked over his shoulder only to see his boys laughing at him. He turned back to Nina. "Oh, so you don't think we could have discussed this shit in private rather than putting all my business out in the street?"

Nina began laughing like a mad woman.

"You already put your business out in the street when you were flaunting your little whore in front of all your niggas. And furthermore, there ain't shit for us to discuss. I want you to get your shit and get the fuck out of my house." Nina pushed pass him, walking towards her truck. All of his boys were staring at her, which really ticked her off. Because they all knew what was going on and yet they came in her house everyday, eating her food and smiling in her face. "And what the fuck are y'all looking at?"

They all turned their heads and looked the other way.

Nina got in her truck and merked off, leaving Cream in the middle of the street looking like an ass next to his keyed up car.

One of his boys jokingly yelled out to him, "Get your shit and get out!" causing a roar of laughter on the block. Cream walked back to the corner, trying to laugh it all off. "You know I ain't going nowhere nigga. All I have to do is buy that big baby a gift and she will be okay."

The loud ringing of the house phone awakened Kennedy. When she reached for it the ringing stopped. She rolled over and as soon as she closed her eyes her cell phone began to ring. She fumbled around the bed until she found it and answered in an irritated voice. "Hello!"

"Dang, girl, where you at?" Nina asked on the other end.

"I was in the state of sleep, a good sleep too. What time is it?"

"It is a quarter to ten."

"Damn, I been sleep for six hours?"

"You was taking all them No-Doze. When you come down off them things you come down hard."

"Tell me about it. What up though?"

"Ain't nothing, packing up Cream's shit."

"Say word."

"Word, my nigga."

"Why?"

"Come to find out, he been messing with some young girl from Jefferson the last six months. He moved her into Lenox Terrace. And now she pregnant. So you know she keyed the Lex because he wants her to have an abortion."

Kennedy sat silently on the phone as Nina told her the story. Actually, she had known about Cream and Tasha's little affair, but had not bothered to tell Nina. Most people would think that was cold hearted. But Kennedy had learned her lesson about telling Nina things she had heard in the street. Nina would go back and tell Cream what she had heard from Kennedy, then take his word over hers. So she stopped telling her anything altogether.

Kennedy's line beeped. "Hold on, Nina, I got another call." She clicked over. "Hello?"

"What up ma? Where you at?"

"Hi Has. I'm home. Hold on right quick; let me get off the other line."

She clicked back over to Nina.

"Yo, Nina, I have to go that's Hassan."

"Oh, so you just gonna hang up with me like that? For that nigga?"

"Come on, Nee, you know it's not like that."

"Go on, Kennedy, you know I'm just messing with you. Handle your B.I. and hit me later."

"Aight, Nina, be careful, and don't let that nigga buy his way back in. I love you, ma. Be easy."

"I love you too, Kennedy. Holla back."

Kennedy clicked back over. "What up Has?"

"You know I was about to hang up."

"My bad. You still coming over?"

"Yeah, I'm still coming over, but can you come get me off my block I already put my truck in the garage for the night."

"That's cool; I'll be there in about thirty minutes. I need to take a shower first."

"Aight, ma. One."

Kennedy got up and slipped off her sweaty clothes then turned up the air conditioner. It was still muggy and humid outside. She took a ten-minute steamy shower, washing away the sticky sweat with peppermint soap.

She felt like a new person after her long nap and refreshing shower. She rubbed her body down in lotion then put on a short pair of gray cotton shorts and a gray fitted tee. She stood in the mirror brushing her hair thinking, *I need a fresh doobie and maybe a relaxer too.* Then she was out the door.

When Kennedy pulled up to Hassan's block. Everyone turned around and tried to figure out who was in the gray X-5 with the gray tints. She rolled down her window and called out to Hassan. "Yo, you coming with me?"

"Yo, Ken, what up? I didn't know that was you, hold up I'm coming."

Hassan's cousin, EB, began questioning him. "Yo who that pretty young thing pushing that X?"

"You remember Kennedy from 141st and eighth."

EB squinted his eyes to get a closer look. "Lil thick Kennedy who used to rap? That's her?"

"Yeah, man, that's her."

"Damn, I didn't know y'all still kept in contact."

"I hadn't seen her in almost two years. I bumped into her last week at the Gucci store, but she was on her way out of town or something."

"You know I could hit that, right?" EB told Hassan with a sly smile on his face.

Hassan just laughed. "Nigga, you couldn't hit that with a bat. Anyway I'm out. Get at me tomorrow."

Hassan exchanged pounds with everyone on the block before going to the truck.

EB walked over to speak to Kennedy. "What up, girl? How you been?"

"I been okay; what about you, EB?"

"I'm straight, you know, doing my thug thizzle."

"Aight then, be easy, my nigga."

Hassan got in and gave her a hug. "What's poppin', Ken? I didn't know who you were pulling up on me like that. I thought you still had the Acura."

"I got rid of that after I had my son."

"Yeah? How's your baby doing?"

"He straight. He down south with my mother I'm going to get him tomorrow."

"That's what's up. What was you doing out in Vegas, vacationing?"

"Something like that."

"Ma, what you out here doing in the world. And don't lie, 'cause I heard you was doing your thing-thing."

"Come on, you know me, Has. And now I got my son so I have to grind harder."

"I feel you. Just be careful you know these streets is ugly."

"Trust me, I know," she replied, voice full of emotion, then shook it off.

"You hungry Has?"

"A little. Why?"

"'Cause I'm going to get something from the Jamaican spot on 45th and Eighth. I haven't went food shopping, so ain't shit to eat at my house."

"That's straight. Get me whatever you getting, as long as it's not pork."

"Boy, you know I don't hardly eat no pork. I'm getting curry chicken, rice and peas, and plantains."

"Get me that and some half and half. Here, is twenty enough?"

"Keep that; It's my treat. You're a guest in my home tonight." She got out of the truck and walked towards the store.

As she walked away, his eyes were fixed on her thick thighs. He just sat and reminisced about how good she was in bed, especially that thing she did with her tongue. Just thinking about it made his dick hard.

The sound of Kennedy opening the door brought him back to reality.

"Damn Has what was you thinking about? You didn't even see me standing here with the bags in my hand."

"I was just thinking about hitting that," he said, slipping his hand between her legs.

At Kennedy's they ate, drank Heinekens, and talked about life. Hassan pulled out a sandwich bag filled with weed. "Ken, you ever smoke purple haze?"

"I tried that shit before, it's strong as hell. I just stick to dro and a little Branson from time to time."

"Well, you 'bout to smoke some of this haze with me."

He pulled out an Optimo cigar, cracked it, emptied the contents, and filled it with the haze. Before they had finished smoking the first blunt, he had already rolled another blunt. Kennedy was only able to take two hits of the second blunt. "That is enough for me. I'm stuck," she said. While getting up and attempting to cross over Hassan, he grabbed her by the hips and pulled her in front of him, caressing her thighs with his hands. He slid his hands under her shorts and massaged her throbbing, moist, warm middle.

"Let me take these shorts off, ma."

She could only nod her head up and down as he removed the shorts. The haze had her gone, and it had been so long since she had slept with anyone. The touch of his hands alone simply made her melt. He stood up; his 6'2 frame towered over her 5'7 body.

He removed his tee shirt, and dropped his shorts and boxers. He pulled her tee over her head, revealing her bare breast. He bent down and began giving her ears and neck wet tongue kisses. Hassan sat back on the couch. He grabbed Kennedy by the thighs and pulled her down on top of him.

She held her breath as she slowly slid onto him, letting out a slight whimper when he was all the way in. She was extra tight after almost a year of no sex. Hassan moaned from the tightness and wetness of her walls. The quicker she began to move, the better it felt to the both of them.

He stood up, never pulling out, and carried her to the bedroom. He laid her on the bed, placing both legs on his shoulders. He pulled halfway out and dropped all the way down, causing her to moan loudly.

As he began to stroke her faster, she bit down on her lip to keep from screaming loudly. She was getting wetter and wetter, and he could feel it.

"Ma, you coming?"

Still unable to speak, she just nodded her head.

"Wait, don't come yet."

He flipped her onto her stomach and entered from the back. He stroked her faster and faster until her body trembled in ecstasy.

"Oh my God, baby," she moaned over and over as she came all over his dick. He pulled out and let off all over her back. Out of energy, he laid on her back gasping for air, and heart racing. Once he caught his breath, he got up and went to the bathroom. A few minutes later he returned with a warm rag. Kennedy lay in the same position unable to move. Hassan cleaned off her back and I between her legs.

"Ken you okay?"

"I'm aight."

"Get up and get under the covers."

She lifted her body as much as she could and crawled under the covers. Hassan got under the covers and wrapped his arms around her.

"Ma that shit was bananas!"

Already half asleep, she responded, "Am I suppose to say thank you?"

"You ain't got to say shit. Just don't get ghost on a nigga again."

"That you don't have to worry about."

Kennedy fell into a deep sleep, still fatigued from the past week. Hassan wasn't tired but he knew she could not go another round. He rolled another blunt and watched television until he fell asleep.

Nina sat on the couch watching episodes of "Sex and the City" she had missed on TiVo. She had bathed the kids and put them to bed hours earlier. She finished packing all of Cream's belongings and had sat them by the front door. It was 2 a.m. and he wasn't home yet.

Around two-forty-five, she heard his keys in the door. Once inside, he saw all his bags. He mumbled to himself, "She can't be serious."

He walked into the living room holding two dozen roses and bags from Chanel. Nina never took her eyes from the screen, even when he tried to start a conversation.

"So you gonna act like you don't see me standing here, huh? Look what I bought you. I got the Chanel sandals and the matching bag that you was looking at."

Nina looked at him, then at the bags and turned her nose up. "I don't want that shit."

"This shit cost three G's"

"So what? Give it to that young bitch. And while you at it, get your shit and take it to her house. My bad; I meant *y'all* house."

"Nina, come off it. It wasn't that serious. That bitch didn't mean nothing to me. I love you only, and I am so sorry I hurt you. Now come over here and give me a hug."

Nina was becoming irritated that he wasn't taking her serious.

"Cream, are you listening to me? Do you understand what I am saying to you? I want you to get your things and get the *fuck* out of my house."

He immediately became aggressive towards her, screaming. "Bitch, I'm not going anywhere! This is my house. I take care of Maddy and them damn boys that ain't even mine! Bitch, you tripping if you think I'm going somewhere!"

"No, nigga, you bugging, 'cause I have never asked you for anything. I got my own paper. And as for Niko and Taylor, I never asked you to support my kids. And everything you do for Madeline, you're supposed to. You're her father. You know what? You are just as pathetic and trifling as Kennedy said you were."

"Kennedy! Oh, so now you listening to that bitch again? Is that who put it in your head to put me out? Since you want to listen to her, see if she's willing to take this ass whipping."

Whap! He smacked Nina, causing her to fall backwards over the top of the couch. She fell on the floor with a loud thump that woke up the boys. They ran into the living room, and saw Cream picking Nina up by her shirt and punching her repeatedly in her face.

Taylor screamed out, "Mommy!"

Between punches and trying to fight back, she answered her oldest son's cry.

"Tay, take your brother go in the room and lock the door."

Taylor grabbed the phone off the hall table and ran in the room with Niko. He nervously dialed Kennedy's phone number.

Kennedy's phone rang five times before she woke up; she looked at the caller ID before answering. She picked up the phone.

"Nina why are you calling me at three in the morning?"

A tearful Taylor answered, her. "Ken, this is Tay."

"Baby, what's wrong?" Kennedy slid from underneath Hassan's arm and sat straight up.

"It's Mommy. Cream is beating her bad." Kennedy jumped out of bed waking up Hassan. "Okay, baby, where are you now?"

"I'm locked in the room with Niko."

"Where is Maddy?"

"She's in her room."

"Listen, Tay, stay in your room. Don't come out until I get there. I will be there in five minutes, okay, baby?"

"Okay, Ken."

"See you in five minutes, bye."

She threw on the first tee shirt and jeans that were in sight.

Hassan asked her, "Where you going, ma?"

"Cream is beating Nina's ass again. The kids just called, terrified. You can stay here as long as want, the slam lock is on the door." Kennedy rumbled through her drawer until she found the spare keys to Nina's apartment. She went under her mattress and pulled out a 9 mm semi automatic handgun. She checked the magazine to make sure it was loaded. Hassan saw the gun.

"Kennedy, what are you taking that for? Are you sure you don't need me to go?"

"Nah, Has, that's okay. I'll call you tomorrow. I'm out."

Against Niko's protest, Taylor cracked the door. He looked out and saw Nina and Cream still going at it. He was still hitting her with hard blows all over her body, but she didn't take them lying down. She fought back as much she could, scratching, kicking, and swinging her arms. She reached onto the coffee table, grabbed an iron candlestick holder, and hit him in the eye, causing him to lose his balance. He fell backwards; she stood up dazed and tried to make it to the bedroom to get her gun. She wasn't quick enough. In one swift movement he was up and right behind her.

He grabbed a hand full of hair, yanking her through the air towards him. He spun her around and began choking her. She wanted to fight back but couldn't. She was too busy trying to remove his hands from her neck.

He released his right hand, pulled back, and hit her with a powerful punch, right between the eyes. The punch packed so much power he could not even hold onto her with his left hand. She fell backwards hitting her head on the steel bar that was affixed to the glass dining table.

Glass shattered everywhere, and blood flowed from Nina's mouth and nose as she lay unconscious Cream was frozen with fear. Out of all of their fights, nothing like this had ever happened. The blood was coming out so fast, and he knew it was more than a busted lip or nose.

He started to panic; he didn't know what to do. He ran to Madeline's room and grabbed her out the bed. He picked up one of the duffel bags that Nina had packed. With Madeline in his arms, he ran down the stairs to the car. He laid Madeline down in the backseat, hopped in the car, and pulled off.

As Kennedy drove up to Nina's building, she saw Cream driving away. She thought to her self, *Good, the drama is over.*

She used her key to get into the building then ran up the stairs. The door to Nina's was ajar; she stepped in and called out, "Nina, baby, are you okay? Taylor called me. Where are you?"

From the corner of her eye, she saw Nina lying on the floor. She ran over to Nina, knelt down beside her, and lifted her head.

"Nina, baby, wake up. It's Kennedy. Taylor, you can come out now; I'm here baby hurry."

Taylor came out and got a surreal view of his mother.

"Tay, baby, I need you to dial 9-1-1. Tell them we need help. Tell them your Mommy has been hurt very bad, and she is not moving."

Niko stood over Kennedy and Nina with his face covered in tears and mucus. "Ken, he took Maddy."

"He did? I didn't see her in the car. Well we'll get her back. Niko, baby, I need you to go get me a glass of water and a wet rag."

Nina started coughing and gagging and more blood came out of her mouth. She looked up at

Kennedy. "Ken-Ken take care of my kids, please. Don't let nobody take them."

"Nina, stop talking like that. You're gonna be okay the ambulance is on the way."

"I can't, Ken. The pain is to bad in my head. I want you take my kids; please promise me."

"I promise, but you're going to be okay; you can't leave me yet. I won't let you get off the hook that easy."

"Tell my kids I love them so much. And I hope I didn't upset you."

Kennedy had tears streaming down her face.

"Ma, I'm not upset with you."

"'Cause you was always right about me. You were the only one who kept it gully with me. I love you."

"I love you too. Now stop talking save your breath."

"Ken, please don't be mad, but I... I can't make it."

Nina's eyes closed a she took her last breath. A cool breeze ran through the room, causing the hair to stand up on the back of Kennedy's neck. She began to shake Nina's lifeless body. "Nina, wake up. No Nina you are not leaving me now. Come on, ma, we have too much to do."

Kennedy wiped the blood from Nina's mouth and tried CPR with no luck; Niko and Taylor looked on, crying as Kennedy continued to talk to Nina. She rocked back and forth with Nina in her arms. "Nina why, why, baby... Why didn't you call me baby? Why didn't you call me? I would have came. I was only playing when I said don't call me."

The paramedics and police rushed through the door. The police took Kennedy to the side for questions. As she answered their questions, to the best of her knowledge, she continued to watch as the paramedics worked on Nina with no success.

Kennedy looked over and saw Niko and Taylor on the couch. Niko had his head buried in Taylor's chest; Taylor was trying to console his younger brother. He was crying just as hard as Niko. Kennedy attempted to wrap up the conversation with the police. "Can we finish this later? The boys they need me."

The short, round lady officer was probably mother. She empathized with Kennedy. "That is perfectly fine. We'll be here for a while, but I need for you to give me a recent picture of Madeline. And we need to speak to the boys once they settle down a little. Is there anyone I can call for you?"

"No, my aunt is on her way here now."

Kennedy went and sat down between the boys, pulled them close and wrapped both arms around them. They sat still as the coroner bagged Nina's body and took her away. Kennedy stared straight ahead as she spoke to the boys. "This is why you never put your hands on a woman. Always honor your mother's memory, and never hit a woman. Promise me and your mother right now you will never hit a woman."

Tearfully they answered, "I promise."

Later that morning, everyone gathered at Karen's house. Out of Kennedy's seven aunts, and her Mother, Karen was the strongest. Whenever something went wrong, she was the one who the family called on. Kennedy was her favorite niece and everyone knew it. She had favored Kennedy ever since Kennedy's childhood, because Kennedy reminded her of her self.

She watched Kennedy from the other side of the living room. She noticed how run down and tired Kennedy looked. She also knew that Nina's passing was going to tear Kennedy to pieces sooner or later. She watched as others attempted to talk with Kennedy and Kennedy would not respond; she would only look at them like they were stupid. Karen decided that it was time for Kennedy to get away from the crowd.

"Kennedy, baby, come on, you need to go lay down."

"I'm aight, Auntie, I just wish she would have called me."

"Sweetie, you can't carry on like this. You can't blame yourself for this one."

Kennedy laid her head on Karen's shoulder and broke into tearful sobs.

"Auntie, you don't understand. We had an argument about Cream when we came back from Vegas. And I told her not to call me the next time he was beating her. I didn't mean it; I just said it in the heat of the moment."

"Baby, I know you didn't mean it, and Nina knew you didn't mean it. You were always there for her, even when the family gave up on her."

"I know, Auntie, but we were more than cousins; she was my sister."

"I know, baby, I know. Have you talked to your mother again?"

"She called me from Auntie Klarice's house. She said Auntie Klarice was in denial."

"I can only imagine what she is going through, losing her oldest child to the hands of that low-life nigga."

"My mommy said they will be here sometime tonight. She was going home to book plane tickets for them and Grandma."

Karen fought back the tears as she looked down at Kennedy, lying in her lap like a child. For the first time, she noticed that Kennedy's dark jeans and hot pink tee shirt was covered in blood.

"Kennedy, let me take you to your house so you can take these clothes off. You need to get away from all these people for a little while."

As they got up to leave, Cream's mother, Vivian, walked through the door, holding Madeline. Kennedy took Madeline out of her arms and hugged her. Glad to have her back safely, she sat back on the couch and placed Madeline on her lap.

Vivian was very humble. She apologized many times and explained how Cream just dropped Madeline off around five a.m. Vivian honestly felt bad and humiliated over Cream's actions, so she decided not to hang around any longer than necessary.

"Maddy, honey, come give Grandma a big hug. I'm getting ready to leave now."

Madeline attempted to get up, but Kennedy wouldn't let her go. For the first time, Kennedy looked up at Vivian. "Miss Vivian, please don't take this the wrong way or don't think I'm trying to disrespect you when I say this. But the next time you talk to your son, you need to tell him his best bet is to turn his self in to the police. Because if me or any of my brothers see him, or Nina's brothers, or our cousins see him, you'll know exactly what my Aunt Klarice is going through right now. But then again, he won't be safe on Rikers, or any jail in the state of New York, will he?" Kennedy smiled coldly and let Madeline go. "Go give your Granny a hug so she can go."

Vivian hugged Madeline quickly and walked so fast to the door, she almost ran.

Kara was the snooty rich know-it-all sister whom no one got along with, especially Kennedy. She looked at Kennedy and shook her head. "Kennedy, you ought to be ashamed, talking to that nice lady like that, after she came over here so humble. I swear you have no couth."

"Kara, take that snooty, I-got-my-masters-degree shit back to Queens and shove it up your tight ass! I'm not for it today, not when my cousin, my sister, my best friend just died in my arms." Kennedy was right in her face. Kara was scared to even breathe.

Karen placed her hand on Kennedy's shoulders and gently pulled her away. "Come on, Kennedy, sweetie, don't do it. She is not even worth it."

Kara was fuming. "Karen, why are you taking her side? She was rude and disrespectful to Vivian, and now me."

Karen stepped up to Kara's face. "I want you to leave her alone. She may have been crass in her approach, but she was right. Vivian knows where her son is, and I didn't appreciate her coming in here with all her self-serving apologies either, despite being glad Maddy was back. Come on, Kennedy, let's go."

"That's okay Auntie, I'll drive myself. I'll take Maddy with me and get her cleaned up too."

She picked Madeline up and walked out of the door, slamming it behind her.

Kennedy placed Madeline in the backseat and strapped her in. She got in the car, put on her seatbelt, but could not move. After a minute or so, she took a deep breath and started the car. She drove down Lenox in a daze, feeling like the world was moving, though *she* wasn't.

She sat at the red light on 139th and Lenox, looking at all the kids in the park playing with not a care in the world. All of their innocent faces were so beautiful, so full of hope. She continued to watch them play, wondering what they would be when they grew up. Her thoughts were interrupted by Madeline's tiny voice.

"Ken-Ken."

"Yes, baby?"

"Can I have an icy?"

Kennedy looked at Madeline, who was watching the kids outside, lined up at the icy cart. "Yeah, lil' mama, I'll get you one by my house after you eat some food. Okay?"

"Okay."

Kennedy turned around in time to catch the light turning green, but Madeline wasn't finished talking.

"Ken-Ken, are you taking me home?"

"We're going to my house right now. Why?"

"I want my Mommy."

Kennedy had not given any thought as to how she was going to explain Nina's death to Madeline. She thought to herself, *how do you tell a two year old she will never see her mother again?*

With tears streaming down her face, she gave the only response she could.

"Baby, I want your Mommy too."

Acknowledgments

Upon the re-release of this book, I decided not to change my acknowledgements in the back because those were my thoughts when this book was written in 2000.

In the last couple of years, things have changed drastically. New people have come in and out of my life. Some people have had a great impact on my life. Others have had none. I am taking this time to acknowledge some people, old and new, whose actions negative or positive have made me better over the last couple of years.

As always, I have to give my Heavenly Father all the praise, glory and thanks. These have been some very trying times. Sometimes I have stepped outside of my faith and yielded to temptation instead of waiting on your Word. Time after time, you have shown mercy on me, even though I am a sinner. Thanks for continuously carrying me in my weakest moments. God, I love you with all that I have. Thanks for your continuous patience. Thanks for the message you have placed on my heart. I will do my best to deliver it. Thanks, your child.

Poppa, you are mommy's strength. Everything I do is done for you. You are so special, and to watch you everyday as you experience new things is so exciting for me. You are so worth the sacrifices, and no one can ever tell you different. I fall deeper in love with you every single time I look into those beautiful, big brown eyes.

My son's father, I am still thankful to you for my child. In a previous printing I said some pretty harsh things towards you. I'm glad we were able to resolve those issues, and put them behind us. Thanks for stepping your game up. I can respect that.

Two of A Kind Publishing, thanks for the love. Brother James Muhammad, you are the best, hands down. Thanks for giving me the chance to express myself without asking me to change who I am. Crystal, you are so Beautiful and you have the biggest heart to match for it. Forget what your husband says; we're going shopping. Big Al thanks for the support, and most of all, the motivation for me to get the job done. This is only the beginning to what is destined to be very prosperous. Let's get that Guape, fam!

Kev "K. Elliot", you have shown me so much love from the door. I thank you so much for that. You are one of my only true friends in the industry. I wish you much success, and don't change anything that you don't want to. F*%$ these industry standards. It's our job to shake shit up anyway!

Shannon Holmes, aka Book Boy, I don't even know where to begin. You are a special person with a heart of gold. Thanks for all the great advice and for protecting me from the woes of this shady industry. I know I can be a hardass and, I know it seems at times that I don't listen to what you say, but I take everything to heart. I just need time to grow into every part of my new life. Thanks for everything, Book Girl.

A special Shout Out to Triple Crown for paving the way and doing it REAL BIG! Vickie, your reputation precedes you. And it's so Gangsta. And certain chicks with whack companies only hate you 'cause they Ain't you. You and Shannon are the last of a rare breed. Y'all want anybody and everybody to eat and get money. That's a great attribute, and your company continues to grow because of it.

Toni Greene, you alone pushed me to the next level out of love. You are the most compassionate publicist in New York City. You have always gone far and beyond your duties to make sure I succeeded. You are truly blessed, and everything is going to pay off in a big way.

Joe Margolis, I know that I am not the best client to work with at times, but thanks for your patience. You and your family are in my prayers.

A very special THANKS to Erica Seppala, of the Nu Day Domestic Violence Shelter, for giving me the boost that I needed at that moment. I promise to help you in the fight against domestic violence in any way I can.

Last but not least, a very special thanks to Sharice Williams, of Seventeen Magazine, for being a driving force behind my new direction.

My family, immediate and extended, thanks for the continued love and support. My thoughts remain the same as said in the back of the book. Rest in peace Uncle Robert, Aunt Bet, and Aunt Ettie V.

My Godmother Peaches Dixon, I have so much love for you. Please forgive me for my absentmindedness. To all the Mothers, especially the single Mothers, I know firsthand how hard your job is. I know it's frustrating, and that kids can tear your nerves down. But please choose your words and actions wisely. Not even kids are promised tomorrow. If anything ever happened to mine, I would give my life to have him back getting on my nerves every day.

One Love

Danielle's (Nesha) Acknowledgments

I would like to first give all praises and thanks to my Lord and Savior Jesus Christ. Through you I can do all things; without you I can do none. Thank you, God for saving me from my own self-destruction by sending me the most wonderful blessing, my son. Kaden Chanze, AKA Butta, AKA Poppa, you are the exclusive love of my life. I cherish the day you were born.

With all my heart, I can honestly say that I never knew love until I met you, and I am so in love with you. You were my one and only inspiration to write this book. I love you so much and I will always be there for you no matter what we go through as you grow into childhood then into manhood.

To my son's father, thanks for my child. Keep your head up; you will be home before you know it.

Denise, my mother, my driving force. Thank you so much for holding me down even when I'm being foolish! You always believed in me when no one else did, that's why I'm about to get you up out that hood and give you that Land Rover too (smile).

Daddy, I know we don't see eye to eye a lot anymore, but I still Love you. I just need for you to understand that I'm a young woman who has seen things that I wish I had not. Things that bring me nightmares, and things that stole my innocence.

Aundi, my baby sis, I love you. Thanks for all the encouragement. Hang in there I know its hard right now, but the road I chose is harder. Darion, baby bro sometimes you have to do things that you don't want to in order to get ahead in life. Regardless of your decision, I got your back, and I love you always.

Lamont, you have been a wonderful big brother, you were never overbearing. Most important, you let me experience life for myself, and I love you for that. Suge, my big sister, who thinks she is my mother also. We have had some very hard times, but I love you no matter what! The tats still on my arm, One Borough (Harlem), One Family, One love! And we're coppin' those twin Benzes (Big Girl Toys.) It's a beautiful look for us this year.

My nieces Kangi, Chataya, Chatiqua, Charlie, and my nephew Donte' auntie loves you. Mommy Verne thanks for treating me like your own and loving me. Special thanks to my grandparents for everything and I still miss you Grandma Louella. I know you're with me everyday especially through that tat on back. Rest In Peace I love you forever. Aunt Teresa thanks for the courage to move on, the friendship, and raising me. Uncle Ant I'm still in the game get at me.

Special thanks to all my aunts and uncles, Patsy, Jackie, Connie, Glo, EZ, Buster, Chuck, Tinker, Tanya and the 100 I didn't name please forgive me. My first cousins Dawn, Nikki, Tanya, Trina, Marco, Big Duke, (Rest in Peace, I miss you) Tresha, Brianna, Trey, Ephram, and Menessah. The rest of y'all know I love you, but it is way too many to name.

Crissy Smith, my sister and my best friend you are so beautiful inside and out. This is our outlet and It is our time Ma!!!!!!!!! My crew Kisha Robison (we're mothers now! Gag), Shakeerah Shuford, (Harlemgirl24 you give me so much love.), and Shanice (finish what you started chic.)

Special shouts to LaQuan Huntley (my big sis), Haaja Kaaba (My overbearing sis), and Rika and Tierra (my little sisters) Rest in peace Mika, Shay -Shay, and Nikki Bolton I wish you were here. Special Thanks to my hairstylist Nikki Long at Imaginations II in Charlotte, NC. Thanks to Cori at Cori's hair and nails.

My two brothers who helped me make this possible Jake Luva (Brooklyn) and Fatz (Harlem) thanks for holding me down over the years. Thanks for all the support, the belief and the advice. Fatz I know I can be greasy but you know I don't mean no harm.

Thanks Shani for being so beautiful, I could not have chosen better God parents than you and Fatz. Big shouts to Snake and Superstar Jewelry Norfolk, VA. Pep and Uptown Jewelers Charlotte, NC. My Philly connection, Shay don't play, Sue, Shamira, and Buddah.

All my Brooklyn people thanks for the love you have shown me, Dre, Troy, and Bernard. Trav thanks for not hating me after the damage. And it is your time to shine baby! J'mel thanks for dropping so many mental jewels on me.

Max Bert Jean Paul, what up ma? Get at your home girl. Danielle Lawson you will make it through my prayers are with you. Shawn from Bed Stuy (smile) in the mean time what do you do? All my family in the Bronx Steve, Michael, Dale, Carolyn, Susan, Kim, and Keyamesha I love you. And I promise to come visit. Kasci we are so unfoolish now! And them chicks can only resemble us ma.

PLEASE STAND UP!!! HARLEM IS IN THE BUILDING!!!!!!!!!!!!!!!!!!!!!!!!!!!!!!!!!! Aunt Sharon, the President, thanks for the guidance and all the love Aunti. Thanks for teaching me the rules, cause it is rules to this shit! I love you kiss Kalief for me and say hi to Shareef and what up to Dee. So much love for that infamous block 141st and 8th.

My home girls Iesha, Tina, and Kim Lyde Love y'all, kiss the kids Monet and Chaquita. Monique ma you still got it. Sha-Sha aka Quanika Mason it's on now. Thanks to Grandma Lena, Auntie Marlene, Auntie BB, Lawanda (my baby sister), Chamya, Paris, Quincy, JJ, and Cathy. Special Thanks to Aunt Gladys, Samantha, and Sade.

Sophie thanks for the late nights, talking about these niggas (who we don't need) and taking tequila shots. Special thanks to Tanya from 144th you are a true friend. Shouts out to Mama, Monica, Katina, and Dawn. Everyone holding down blocks on 8th Ave. The entire Drew Hamilton, the Polo Grounds, The All Stars (Lucci and Amin), DFerg, 3 Stoogez (Keep the parties coming) and of course The world famous Rucker.

Big June I have so much love for you! Everybody in Lincoln, good looking out. My favorite brother Kayo, thanks for all the love you have shown me, thanks for helping ease the emotional pain and making sure I wrote my rhymes while I was pregnant. (Smile) Jade you are special to me ma with your fly ass.

Shouts out to Moses (thanks for the meals) and so much love to Jared. KFC, you still get mad love. You always asked me, was I still writing my rhymes. I kept writing and it got me to my first book! I am so happy for you right now you are definitely doing your thing- thing Pa. (Oh Boy!)

Big shouts to the Hill, my big brother Monte (stop smacking niggas be easy), Security, The O, and the barbershop. Thanks to Don Diva and FEDS magazine. Big shouts to Harlem's Finest. All my favorite spots, the fish store 140th and 7th, Spoonbread Too, Jimmy's in Harlem (and the Bronx!), Apollo Express, Mannas, Mony's, Peoples Choice Jamaican food, M&K's, 1 fish 2 fish, the third park 143rd and 8th, and Esplanade Gardens.

Big up to Cousin A, Cee Bee (you're in my prayers) and Buster. Thanks Marisols hair salon on

Amsterdam for keeping that doobie tight. Top's African hair braiding on 125th and St. Nick.

A sincere Thanks and I Love you to the Entire New York City for all the love. All the victims of September 11th you are in prayers everyday. All my people on lock, I will not put ya names out there (I don't need no visits from the feds) but you are in my prayers. Get at me so I can put some money on them books. If I forgot anyone, please forgive me and I will catch you in the next book, Grindin' for Keeps..... A Harlem Story.